CURSED CITY

A SHADOW DETECTIVE NOVEL

WILLIAM MASSA

CRITICAL MASS PUBLISHING

PROLOGUE

It's official, Blaire thought. *I hate camping.*

Her teeth chattered in the frigid tent. No matter how much she tried to cocoon herself inside her sleeping bag, she couldn't get warm.

The camping trip had sounded like a romantic idea when Eric first brought it up to her, three months earlier. Her mind had filled with visions of hiking through a fairy tale forest and snuggling up to her sweetheart under the stars. The reality was much less pleasant.

It had begun to rain as soon as they unpacked their gear and hit the hiking trails. Somehow they managed to set up their tent despite the biting wind and incessant downpour. Unable to start a fire, they snacked on tasteless protein bars, which she washed down with a bottle of wine.

Talk about a classy combo.

Blaire was thankful she'd had the foresight to bring some alcohol along for the trip, despite Eric's protests. He tended to be sober to a fault. The wine warmed her for a bit, but its soothing effects had long worn off.

Within minutes of slipping into the tent, Eric nodded off. Blaire wasn't so lucky, and she'd spent the last two hours worrying about every random sound outside. God, what she would've given for the wail of a police siren or the sound of someone rummaging through the dumpster below their apartment. Unlike Eric, who grew up on a farm, Blaire was a true city kid. Her idea of roughing it was to take the subway instead of an Uber.

She tried to pass the time by reading a book on her Kindle, but the frigid conditions made it hard to concentrate. Besides, a horror novel was a lot more entertaining when you were safe and snug in your apartment. In the wilderness, stories of mad killers stalking innocent victims lost much of their appeal.

This was going to be a long night.

Making matters worse was her pressing need to relieve herself. She shuddered at the thought of untangling herself from her sleeping bag, leaving the relative safety of their tent, and finding some nearby tree under which to do her business.

She tried to ignore her physical discomfort, but after another restless hour of staring at the tent's ceiling while obsessing over the latest hoot or cracking branch, she couldn't hold it any longer. Either she braved the woods or she peed her pants.

The thought made her turn red with embarrassment and immediately unzip her sleeping bag. She would just have to be quick.

As Blaire crawled out of the tent, she promised herself that this would be her first and last camping adventure. If Eric wanted a girl who could tough it out in the wild, he'd have to look elsewhere.

The night air raked her exposed skin as she stumbled to her feet. Breath clouding before her, arms tightly wrapped around her chest, she scrambled toward the trees. The wet ground slurped under her shoes.

After a chilly minute of frantic searching, she located a spot that was private yet close enough to their tent. She took a deep breath, slipped her jeans to her knees, and dropped to her haunches. Seconds later, blissful relief followed.

For a moment, she blocked out the relentless cold and the sound of her emptying bladder drowned out all the spooky nocturnal noises. Mercifully. Once finished, she pulled up her pants and turned back to their shelter. About fifteen feet separated her from the blue tent, the only pale hint of color in the dark forest. Its trees cast menacing shadows as the pale moonlight shafted through the thick canopy above.

Blaire steeled herself for a quick sprint to the tent. Her limbs felt stiff from the cold, but she knew she could do this. She was just about to take her first step when a droplet of something wet pelted her face.

Oh great, don't tell me it's about to rain again.

When four more drops hit her in quick succession, she realized the liquid felt hot against her skin. She wiped away the wetness pearling on her forehead and studied her hands. Even in the dim moonlight, she could clearly see the crimson smeared across her fingers.

It was fresh blood.

Still too stunned to feel any real fear, Blaire looked up and gasped.

A few feet above her, the severed head of a deer stared back at her with empty eyes.

Someone had decapitated the animal and mounted its head on the tree branch above. The ragged state of the poor creature's neck suggested that its head was torn right off its body.

What kind of monster would do such a thing?!

As Blaire took a step back, a mad cackle burst forth from the dark trees. Terror rippled up her spine and shook Blaire from her fear-frozen state. She exploded into motion, barely aware of crossing the distance between the trees and their tent, ripping the zippered flap open, and crawling inside. It felt as though one moment fear held her in its icy grip and the next she was pressing her frozen face against Eric, shaking him awake. "Wake up," she hissed, voice quivering.

"Someone's out there."

A groggy Eric blinked at her, still half-asleep. Before she could offer an explanation, another peal of crazed laughter filled the night, jolting her beau wide awake.

Blaire scrambled to zip the tent closed. "Oh my God," she breathed.

"What's happening?"

She caught a fleeting glimpse of a black shape outside their tent, followed by a rush of violent motion. The next moment, the tent collapsed on top of them. The stranger outside must've torn the guy-lines out of the ground. Blaire and Eric cried out in panic as the world inside the tent went topsy-turvy. The assailant was now dragging it over the bumpy forest floor with both Blaire and Eric still inside. She clung to Eric with all her might while the hard ground bit into their backs.

The violent forward momentum stopped, and for a moment she felt relieved. Then the tent went airborne. Blaire realized with horror that the shadowy figure must've thrown one of the ropes over a branch and was now lifting them upward like animals caught in a snare. The tent's fabric stretched under their weight, but it didn't rip. They swung back and forth, arms and legs entangled.

A deep wound opened in the tent's fabric, shredding it from top to bottom. Moonlight seeped through the gutted material as their phantom attacker stood before them, at last revealed.

The monstrous creature glaring back at Blaire defied rational thought. Her terrified scream erupted into the night but was quickly drowned out by another burst of inhuman laughter.

1

Death lurked in the dark forest.

The signs were everywhere, and you didn't have to be a seasoned paranormal investigator to pick up on them. An unearthly stillness had settled over the landscape, reminding me that I was the sole living creature foolish enough to brave these parts. The animals that inhabited the woods had all fled. Shadows chased the sunlight shafting through the heavy canopy, and the sky above was the color of melted lead. The syrupy air felt heavy and cloying, as if some strange force was sucking the oxygen from it.

Up ahead, the terrain became more challenging. The trees were taller and more foreboding, the under-brush thicker. Once solid ground was transformed now into a swamp by the unending rain. Scaly trunks and winding, overgrown roots threatened to trip me up, while branches reached out with malevolent intent. With each step, the chilling certainty grew: the forest had declared war against me.

No, not the forest, I reminded myself, *but the evil hiding within its deepest shadows.*

Undeterred, I pressed onward, knowing I was closing in on my quarry.

Most people with a healthy survival instinct would've turned back. Unfortunately, in my line of work, one didn't get the luxury of walking away from danger. Ever since my family was murdered by demons twenty-one years ago, I've dedicated my life to fighting the forces of darkness. My name is Mike Raven, and I hunt monsters.

And sometimes they hunt me.

Today was one of those days.

I paused as my eyes landed on the shredded tent wrapped around one of the trees ahead. Torn strands of blue fabric flapped in the wind like a war-ravaged flag.

Both campers and hikers had gone missing over the last few weeks. Attempts by local law enforcement to comb the woods had come up empty. It was as if the great forest had swallowed nineteen souls whole, only leaving behind a few tattered remnants of their gear.

People disappear every day, but the inverted penta-grams and other occult paraphernalia found near the campsites suggested a supernatural angle to these particular vanishings. Detective John Kove, a former city cop familiar with my reputation as a problem solver for strange cases, had reached out to me about this one. His call had come at the perfect time. A surprising lull in paranormal activity back in the city made me jump at the chance for some action in the countryside.

But it was already turning into the field trip from hell.

As I stood there examining the blood-spattered fabric, little of my appetite for adventure remained. I knew there wouldn't be a happy ending to the story of these missing campers. All I could hope for at this point was to track down the rampaging beast and prevent it from claiming more innocent victims.

I did have a theory about what sort of evil I might be facing here. My research had unearthed information related to an old legend. More than two hundred years earlier, during the winter of 1879, a witch by the name of Mercy Blackmore was banished to these woods and left to starve as punishment for practicing black magic. For centuries, the Blackmore Witch's evil had remained dormant.

Until now.

I looked up from the torn tent and my blood turned to ice.

The circle of barren trees around me had changed while my attention was focused on the victims' shredded tent. Missing person posters now hung from the skeletal trees ahead, the nineteen dead campers staring back at me from their positions in this unholy shrine. Snapshots taken during happier times showed off smiling faces in black and white. The fliers promised substantial rewards for any information about the lost souls in question.

The sight was both heartbreaking and infuriating. This witch was mocking me. I balled a hand around the tent's blood-caked fabric, anger rising within me.

I will put a stop to this, I thought.

Take your best shot, fool!

The voice invading my thoughts was both human and not of this world.

Without warning, the missing person posters ignited into flames and then turned to ash. Burned air singed my lungs.

Almost immediately, the demon-inflicted scar on my chest lit up with a fresh, sharp pain, a clear indicator that black magic was at work here. When the demons slaughtered my parents, the talons of one of the foul beasts had slashed my skin. The wound took months to heal and the scar served as a reminder of the evil that dwelled within the hidden corners of our world. For some reason, the demon's mark tended to become inflamed in proximity to agents of the dark arts. It heightened my awareness of the paranormal in more ways than one, giving me a sixth sense of sorts.

At the moment, my old wound was itching something fierce.

Heart hammering with growing terror, I advanced into the encroaching darkness. After about a hundred feet, I slowed my pace. A broken-down, overgrown cabin stood revealed. Moss and other vegetation tattooed its walls, fusing the forest with the man-made structure.

My demon's mark throbbed. This had to be the origin point of the area's unnatural energy. According to the police reports, the first group of missing hikers planned to stay at a cabin. Was this the cabin in question? Lt. Kove and his fellow officers had failed to locate the structure, even after numerous searches.

The witch must've magically cloaked the place somehow. Only someone whose life had been touched by the supernatural could penetrate her black magic veil.

Someone like me.

My hand slipped underneath my trench coat and closed around the handle of a pistol. The wooden grip felt hot to the touch as I drew *Hellseeker*.

Gifted to me by John Skulick, the demonologist who

had been my mentor since my parents' murder, the holy weapon gave off a spectral green glow. This was one more indicator that evil infused the air. Cast from the broken blade of a magical demon-slayer sword, the pistol was at least forty years old and looked to the untrained eye like an early model Beretta. Bullets fired from *Hellseeker* could destroy most supernatural monsters. Vampires, shifters, demons and ghosts of all kinds feared this magical gun.

I hoped that *Hellseeker* would be able to put an end to the infernal Mercy Blackmore. Emboldened by the weight of the weapon in my hand, I approached the cabin.

It seemed...*alive* somehow. The crumbling building kept expanding and contracting in a subtle manner, as if the structure was the dark, pulsating heart of this accursed forest. An ancient evil dwelled within those walls.

I could only pray I'd be a match for it.

My mud-encrusted boot shot out at the wooden door in a determined kick. It gave way with a creak. Darkness filled the entrance, which gaped like a black wound in the structure's side.

Something stirred in there.

For a moment, a panicked voice inside my mind piped up, urging me to turn around and start running. A palpable terror clawed its way through my body and choked the breath from my lungs.

Not an unreasonable response, considering the lethal power lurking within the witch's domain.

I fought this rising weakness, drawing on the memory of my parents' faces. Their smiles. Thinking about my folks made the old anger well up. It burnt with the same intensity as the demon's mark on my chest and swept the fear aside.

Empowered by my rage, I strode into the cabin. The glow from *Hellseeker* carved warm patches of light from the tomblike darkness. Thick roots and dense shrubbery had infested the building's interior as nature reclaimed what was rightfully hers. Unwholesome foliage spread across the wooden walls and stone floor like a metastasizing cancer.

Gun up, I advanced. A strange calm fell over me. I was eager to face my enemy, eager to find justice for the witch's victims.

"Help me."

A woman's voice drifted through the air, barely more than a whisper.

My eyes narrowed as I peered into the darkness. A young woman stared back at me with haunted eyes. It took me a long moment to recognize her. This was one of the missing campers. The horrors of the last few days had eroded her youthful good looks; the drawn, emaciated features before me were just a shadowy reflection of her once-stunning beauty. The poor girl hunched on a chair, hands secured behind her back with thick, ugly vines that had sprouted from the ground.

Cynical bastard that I am, I hadn't expected to find any survivors. I lowered my weapon and took a step toward her.

I was almost upon the hapless victim when a sharp pain once again tore into my chest. My scar burned as if the demon's biting nail were piercing my flesh right now, rather than ten years ago.

I froze and my face grew cold. I knew what this meant. I knew what I had to do.

I raised *Hellseeker*.

Leveled it at the terrified, traumatized woman in the chair.

And pulled the trigger.

2

Reality sped up the instant I unleashed the wrath of the blessed weapon. The helpless expression on the woman's face gave way to a cold glare of unbridled hatred. Her restraints vanished into thin air as she hurled herself to the ground. The move saved the witch's unholy life, but she wasn't fast enough to completely avoid my bullet. A piercing shriek, more animal than human, echoed through the cabin—*Hellseeker* had found its target. Black blood exploded from the witch's arm moments before the cabin's shadows swallowed her.

My pistol is a formidable weapon in my ongoing battle against all things that go bump into the night. But it's not enough for *Hellseeker* to graze a supernatural foe. A shot to the head or heart is needed to put an end to a creature of darkness. I'd wounded the witch, but she was far from being defeated.

In other words, all I had managed to do was tick off Mercy Blackmore. *Great.*

An invisible force seized me and a wave of deadly cold slammed into my chest, taking my breath away. I knew all too well what that meant. The witch had cast a spell on me. The only reason I was desperately gasping for air instead of exhaling my internal organs was due to the protective pentagram-shaped ring on my finger, the *Seal of Solomon.* Another helpful tool in my battle with the forces of darkness.

I'm no wizard. When I first embarked on my quest to hunt monsters, I'd naturally toyed with the idea of mastering magic. Why not, right? If you comb through tome after tome of arcane occult knowledge, you have to wonder if there might be a way to put it all to good use. After all, you have to fight fire with fire, right? Wrong! Only a fool would dabble with such forces, as Joe liked to remind me all the time.

You play with fire, you're liable to set the whole goddamn world ablaze.

If you're lucky.

To quote my mentor once again, "Magic corrupts, and black magic is an express ticket to Hell." Human nature and magic represent a recipe for disaster. Even if you start off with the best of intentions, odds are good that using magic will eventually corrupt you—or get you killed.

I'd faced enough mad sorcerers in my day to know this to be true, all of them fallen idealists who'd succumbed to the dark siren call of unholy power. There were no good wizards outside fairy tales—or at least I hadn't made their acquaintance yet. Our primate brains are poorly equipped to handle the high price that comes with such power.

That said, only an idiot takes a knife to a gunfight. Mastering spells that bend reality may be a sure shot to becoming a big bad, but using magical artifacts to battle monsters is another story. Without *Hellseeker*, my protective ring and my other weapons, I wouldn't be much good in a fight against a bloodthirsty vampire or ravenous shapeshifter.

Pistol blazing, I scrambled away from the menacing silhouette.

Even though I was still among the living, I felt like I'd gone a couple of rounds in a vicious MMA bout. A bulletproof vest can save your life, but the bruises sure as hell will keep you from catching a good night's sleep for days afterward. Magical defenses are a lot like that. The *Seal of Solomon*, for example, could ward off one or two magical attacks, but the ring would soon become useless under a sustained assault.

I had to defeat Mercy Blackmore before she cast another spell.

My mind went blank as the witch lurched at me from the darkness. No trace of the human mask remained now. The creature was the stuff of nightmares. Bloodshot eyes leered back at me from a ghostly white face cratered and crumpled by the passage of time. Gray hair clung to the pale scalp in heavy, dirt-caked clumps. Thankfully, layers of tattered black rags covered the witch's grotesquely distorted body.

She pounced. I stifled a curse as stained, razor-sharp teeth tore at my outstretched arm. I fell, and *Hellseeker* went flying.

Fantastic! A two-hundred-year-old granny from hell was trying to kill me, and I was unarmed.

Not good. Not good at all.

Mercy Blackmore pinned me to the floor, her fingers sprouting long nails that would have made Wolverine envious. I rolled aside, and not a second too soon, as those razor-sharp claws plunged into the moss-covered floor where my head had been a mere moment earlier. The witch-demon let out a guttural roar of frustration.

She was really pissed now.

I guess that made two of us.

Blood roaring in my ears, I stumbled to my feet and combed the floor for my pistol. I had a feeling that if I remained without it, I wouldn't walk away from the witch's next attack. Luck favored me and I spotted *Hellseeker* just five feet away. I dove for the weapon and held back a cry of triumph as my fingers closed around the blessed ivory grip. Better not to tempt fate with a victory dance.

Adrenaline pumping, I spun around, gun ready and...

Found only the empty cabin waiting for me.

A beat later, a nearby window shattered as the witch fled through it. I resisted the impulse to unload *Hellseeker* into the encroaching darkness. Each bullet was precious. Wasting my ammo so I could feel like a badass was unacceptable.

Despite being hit, Mercy Blackmore was as dangerous as ever—if not more so. Nothing fights as viciously as a wounded beast.

I sucked in a deep gulp of air and made my way toward the shattered window. Peeking through the jagged maw of glass I scanned the creepy stand of trees, which stretched out behind the cabin.

A trail of black blood showed me the way Mercy must've gone. The witch was hurt, angry, and gathering her strength for the inevitable counterattack. My scar pulsed and throbbed dully, reminding me that this battle was far from over.

Through the window I went.

Once outside, I took a couple of hesitant steps, my eyes adjusting to the gloom. Where was the witch hiding?

There was something odd about the skeletal trees just ahead. For a surreal moment, they looked like distorted human forms.

I gasped.

Something was staring back at me from a hollow in the nearest tree. A human eye flicked back and forth, shiny with mad terror. My heart sank as I studied the cove of trees more closely. Further inspection confirmed my worst suspicions. I had found the missing campers.

Cursing the wretched monster responsible for this, I approached the first tree. No wonder the branches had reminded me of arms—at one point in time they'd actually been human limbs.

Jesus.

Blackmore's infernal magic had stripped the unfortunate souls of their humanity, fusing flesh with wood. Being drained by a vampire or mauled by a were struck me as a preferable fate to this slow, torturous decay. Growing fury threatened to cloud my thinking.

This is why Blackmore had led me into her horror

garden. The witch must've anticipated my reaction, knowing how the grisly sight would throw me off. Anger can be fuel during a battle, but getting emotional always leads to mistakes. The witch hoped to rattle me so I'd slip up. I wasn't going to oblige. After all, this wasn't my first rodeo with evil.

"Please, help me," whispered a voice.

Did the witch really think I would fall for this trick again? But something was different this time. My scar didn't react. Whoever was calling me, it wasn't the Blackmore Witch.

I scanned the ground and saw a dirt-streaked face looking up at me. To my surprise, I recognized her. It was the same young woman the witch impersonated back in the cabin.

Hope bloomed.

Please, just let me save one.

She'd been buried in a shallow grave. No, not buried —*planted.* I knelt before the woman and started digging like a madman. Roots had enveloped her body but hadn't fused with her skin yet, the transformation evidently beginning its first phase. From the looks of it, I had arrived just in the nick of time.

Pulling out the demon-slaying dagger I'd acquired in India six months earlier while hunting a murderous werepanther, I began sawing away at the roots. Sweat poured down my face and I choked at the salt of my own perspiration. Muscles stretched taut, I was able at last to pull the woman out of the ground.

Initially her wobbly legs failed to support her weight, but with time her body would recover. Whether her mind would follow was another story. Her lost gaze suggested that she was in deep shock; a little girl trapped in a nightmare.

I retraced my steps from the woods, half carrying the dazed girl. My desire to pursue the Blackmore Witch was not as pressing as getting this young woman to safety. As we neared the edge of the unholy grove, one of the trees spoke. It was the one I'd first noticed, and that single, panicked eye was now fixed on us.

"*Blaire*?" a strangled voice asked, just audibly.

The young woman at my side shuddered. "Eric," she whispered, burying her face in my shoulder.

My stomach clenched as she gave a name to the hapless soul caught in mid-transformation between man and tree. I suddenly recalled more about the most recent missing campers. They were a couple: Blaire and Eric.

I bit my lip as the full horror sank in. The witch had wanted Blaire to witness her boyfriend's slow transformation, knowing that once Eric's suffering was over, she'd be next.

Unbridled hatred welled up inside me. The witch fed off the terror and despair of her victims. I was itching for a rematch now, eager to make her pay for what she'd done.

I would get my chance soon enough.

"Please...kill me," the voice inside the tree begged. I knew help had come too late for poor Eric. I raised *Hellseeker*, aimed it at the tree hollow, and pulled the trigger.

One shot was all it took to end the camper's hellish suffering.

The tree blackened and its branches crumbled to dust. Seconds later, only a pile of ash remained.

Blaire's body heaved with tears and she feebly struck at me, distraught. I tried in vain to calm her. I'd put her boyfriend out of his misery, and she instinctively hated me for it.

I never said monster-hunting was an easy gig.

A cackle echoed through the forest. The Blackmore Witch, her laughter mocking my efforts.

A ripple passed through the rows of trees, and the other transformed campers jerked into motion. One by one, the tree monsters pivoted toward us, an eerie phalanx of wooden golems coming to life.

I cursed under my breath as Blackmore's haughty laughter intensified around us. There were seventeen of the monsters. *Hellseeker* held only fifteen bullets—and I'd already used half of them. Even if every one of them was a kill shot, we'd still be outnumbered five to one. The wooden killers under the witch's control would easily overrun us. We had to get out of here. Now. I fired at the two closest tree-beasts and they collapsed into piles of dust the way Eric had.

Legs pumping, I ran back to the shelter of the cabin, Blaire at my side. She kept pace with me, moving with an urgency that surprised me. The woman was a survivor. Despite all she had endured, she wanted to live. Thank God for small miracles.

Back inside, I slammed the door shut and pulled a heavy wooden chair in front of it. It wouldn't stop the tree golems, but it might slow them down long enough to buy us a few precious seconds.

I surged toward the nearest window and fired into the night. Two more of the incoming monsters dropped. Two fewer golems to worry about, but I was also down two more bullets. How long could I hold them back? I feared it was just a matter of time before they tore us to pieces. Unless...

My eyes widened. Pale beams of moonlight lanced the cabin's broken window, revealing the stone fireplace that dominated one wall. A metal cauldron hung suspended within it.

I took my first step toward the fireplace just as the tree-golems slammed against the front door. Blaire jerked and whimpered. Dread also held me in its tight grip, but I refused to give in to my emotions.

I reached the fireplace and examined the cauldron more carefully. As expected, the cauldron was hot to the touch despite the fact that no fire burned beneath it. A quick survey revealed strange glyphs and markings across the pot's surface. Inside, a red liquid bubbled, heated by some supernatural source of energy.

The moment I touched the cauldron, images popped into my mind. Another side effect of the mark on my chest. Ever since the demon-inflicted injury, I can pick up psychic impressions from certain objects and even see the spirits of the deceased. In my vision, I saw a group of kids in the cabin, their laughter echoing in my head. It was a psychic glimpse into the past. Soon, I knew, their joy would transform into abject terror, but right now they still believed they'd live forever.

It must have been cold in the cabin. The girl shivered and hugged her shoulders. While the young men goofed around, she knelt by the hearth and tried to start a fire. She heaved the cauldron aside, grimacing. As she flicked a lighter over a meager pile of sticks and moss, she let out a sharp curse. Blood was dripping from a scratch on her palm, where the jagged lip of the cauldron had grazed her skin. The blood sizzled as it struck the flames...

I pulled back from the iron kettle as if stung, shaken by the power of my vision. Damn!

I now understood what had happened here. The campers' efforts to warm the icy cabin had brought forth an ancient evil. This cauldron was Mercy Blackmore's link to our world, and the girl's blood had acted as a ritual sacrifice to call her forth. If I could break this connection, maybe the witch's spirit would return to whatever hell she'd dwelled in for the last few centuries.

Blaire's scream thrust me back to reality. My eyes widened as the door exploded off its hinges. A swarm of tree golems invaded the cabin. Moving swiftly, they circled our position in an ever-tightening band of approaching death.

I turned *Hellseeker* away from the incoming attackers and leveled my pistol at the cauldron. Vibrations rattled the floor and the Blackmore Witch's shriek of dismay reverberated through the cabin. Judging by her reaction, she knew what I was going to do.

About time this bitch realized just who she was messing with.

My lips twisted into a dark grin as I aimed my magical gun at the cauldron and fired.

Hellseeker's bullet slammed into the iron cauldron,

and for a beat, all the glyphs lit up with a fiery red light. The air hummed with supernatural power as a series of cracks webbed the pot's surface. Then the cauldron shattered—and so did the circle of tree golems around us.

Outside, the Blackmore Witch's wail of dismay died down, her deadly reign over the forest broken. The temperature was still below freezing in the cabin, but the world already felt like a warmer place.

3

The forest had lost most of its menacing quality when we made our way back to my car. The unnatural gloom had lifted, sunlight once again shining through the foliage. The sound of chirping birds filled the air. Even the trees looked healthier and less stunted by the choking vines that had thrived in the unholy aura of the witch's cabin. With the dark spell shattered, the world was reverting back to normal.

The same couldn't be said for Blaire. We didn't speak as we walked, both of us too exhausted for small talk. The poor girl kept stealing furtive glances back and forth, as if each new sound from the forest were fraught with danger. I didn't judge her. She'd experienced horrors beyond the imagination of most people.

I had parked my black Equus Bass 770 about half a

mile away, in one of the dirt spaces near the trailhead. The jet-black, two-door modern-day muscle car sported a supercharged 640 HP V8, could reach top speeds of 200 mph and boasted a 0-to-60 miles-per-hour time of 3.4 seconds. The vehicle channeled the beauty and ferocious power of the legendary muscle cars of the '60s and '70s, drawing inspiration from the old Ford Mustang fastback and the Dodge Challenger. This baby would make even Batman or James Bond jealous.

Blaire shot me a panicked look when I opened the passenger door.

"It's alright," I said. "I'm just giving you a lift to the nearest police station." The words seemed to ease her concerns somewhat, and she reluctantly took a seat in my car. I had saved her life, but I was still a stranger to her. A stranger who battled nightmares. Not exactly the type of guy you'd want to go on a joyride with.

I slipped behind the wheel. A number of wards and protective sigils had been etched across the vehicle's tinted windows. Any supernatural entity trying to breach my wheels would be in store for a nasty surprise. My gut told me we were in the clear, but you never know. The forces of darkness have a way of catching even the most seasoned monster hunter off guard.

I started the engine and eyed Blaire. "I know you've

been through hell and back, but you're safe now. I promise."

My words failed to ease the tension from her body. I couldn't blame her for not trusting me. I wasn't exactly a knight in shining armor. Battling demons took its toll in more ways than one, and in me the cracks were showing. Let's just say I didn't look like someone you'd want to run into in a dark alley—or a brightly lit street, for that matter.

My beard gave me an intimidating quality, which was further enhanced by my well-worn, tattered trench coat. Heavy bags usually lined my eyes, and my smile lines appeared deeply etched in the milky gray daylight. I was twenty-nine going on forty. My brown hair showed signs of white, especially in the sideburns, and I guessed that my little dance with the Blackmore Witch added a few more silver strands to my growing collection. Quick monster hunter fact: melatonin levels are affected when supernatural entities try to skin you alive. Who knew?

I popped open the glove compartment, pulled out one of the best multivitamins on the market and washed down three of them with a piss-warm Red Bull. I offered some to Blaire as if they were breath mints. She gratefully accepted. *Smart girl.* We were both depleted.

I put the car in drive and focused on the trip ahead. It took less than half an hour of winding forest roads to reach the nearest town. My destination was a rustic three-story brick building fronted by lush trees. This police station shared little in common with the squalid urban counterparts I normally frequented.

Lt. John Kove and two fellow officers emerged from the structure as Blaire and I walked toward the main entrance. The good lieutenant wore a sober expression. The fact that I was returning with only one of the missing hikers told him everything he needed to know.

Kove's men draped a blanket over Blaire's shivering shoulders. Would the traumatized young woman ever be the same again? Most people who survived supernatural horrors ended up being scarred for life. Trust me, I know from personal experience. Hopefully Blaire would somehow beat the odds and not become another grim statistic.

"What happened out there, Raven?" Kove asked. Despite his burly six-foot-two frame, he appeared smaller since I'd last spoken to him, his shoulders hunched. This case had weighed heavily on him. Maybe he didn't like what he saw on my face, because he added, "On second thought, better keep it to yourself. I can't put any of this shit in my report, anyway."

Ignorance is bliss.

A melancholic note had crept into Kove's voice, his eyes growing distant as he stared off somewhere over my shoulder. "You know, I moved out here to get away from the craziness of the city. It's happening all over again, isn't it?"

I shook my head, though I couldn't be certain. In fact, I'd asked myself the same question recently, but I sensed that Kove needed to hear something reassuring at this weak moment. He remembered all too well the way supernatural activity had escalated in the city, two years earlier.

Now might be a good time to bring up why I haven't disclosed the name of my current place of residence and keep referring to it as "the city." You may wonder why I'm being vague about geography and won't provide identifying details. Well, there's a good reason for that. The less you know, the better. Trust me on that. I'd rather not have a group of amateur monster hunters descend on my home turf.

Want the gist of it? My city and the surrounding countryside–numerous suburbs and small towns–are cursed.

A little less than two years ago, Skulick and I had come to the city to stop a doomsday cult from opening a gateway into Hell–just another day on the job. Sadly, we were only partially successful in stopping the Crimson Circle's ritual. On the bright side, we prevented the end of the world. But their ritual hadn't been a complete bust. It opened a rift between the city and the dark dimension. With the barrier between the two worlds no longer able to do its job, the city became a nexus for unholy creatures and paranormal horrors. It turned the whole area into a hotspot for supernatural activity.

A Cursed City.

Working the city's murder beat at the time of the breach, Kove got a front-row seat for the craziness. To his mind, as soon as Skulick and I appeared on the scene his city went to Hell—literally. Each week brought another new occult murder case or rampaging paranormal creature. As special consultants to the police, my partner and I had our hands full.

Of course, that was before the accident that put Skulick in a wheelchair. During our investigation of a haunted hotel, a vengeful spirit caught Skulick off guard and dropped him out a window. The three-story fall should've killed the demonologist, but Skulick wasn't the sort to go gentle into that good night.

Not long thereafter, Kove decided that a change of scenery was in order and traded the blood-filled alleys of the Cursed City for the pastoral beauty of this idyllic small town. Nothing terrible could happen out here, right? But monsters don't respect county lines. This latest case served as a sharp reminder that there was no true safe haven left. The city might be Spook Central, but Hell's terrifying influence was spreading beyond its limits at an alarming rate. Swift and merciless, evil could strike anywhere.

Thinking about the Crimson Circle and the creatures their blind fanaticism had unleashed must've darkened my expression, because Kove decided to change the subject.

"How's Skulick holding up?"

"You know how stubborn he can be. The man is a fighter. He's hanging in there, but he hates being stuck in a wheelchair."

Kove nodded. He didn't press me for the grisly details about the thing that almost killed my partner. There are two types of people in this world: those who face the darkness head-on, and those who would rather not know about a supernatural war being fought behind the scenes. Kove belonged to the latter group and intended to keep it that way. I didn't blame him; I even envied him sometimes. I'd never had a chance to ignore the threat of the underworld. That, along with everything else, was taken from me the night my parents were killed.

"You know how to get a hold of me if you ever need my services again," I said, extending my hand to shake.

Kove smiled, but his eyes told me he hoped he'd

never see me again. That would mean things were going pretty well out here.

I regarded Blaire one final time as the cops whisked her inside. Her eyes looked about a hundred years older than the rest of her, haunted by the sight of things that no mortal should ever have to face.

I recognized that expression. I saw it every time I peered in the mirror.

4

The gothic skyline of my adopted metropolis rose before me, the lights of its majestic buildings twinkling in the nighttime shadows. Like many major urban centers, the city has a reputation for being a place that never sleeps. Some of the hippest, most famous restaurants and clubs in the country can be found within its urban canyons, and its late-night delights draw visitors from all around the world.

I pulled off the freeway, shot down the exit ramp and tore through a series of deserted alleys. The glamour of the glittering downtown gave way to blocks of abandoned industrial warehouses. Maybe one day in the near future gentrification would turn this area into a hotspot for hipsters and artists, but at the moment it was still a broken wasteland of failed industry and a mecca for the city's homeless population.

I zipped past sidewalks crowded with tents, where forgotten souls wrapped in tattered rags shuffled along the otherwise empty streets like an army of the undead. This was skid row on steroids.

Home, sweet home.

After another fifteen minutes of crumbling structures and rat-infested alleys for scenery, our four-story loft building jumped into view. This former warehouse served as both our living space and our command center in the war against the supernatural. Sensors registered my approach and a gate rumbled open, allowing me to pull into the underground parking structure.

I couldn't see them from inside my car, but a number of surveillance cameras recorded my approach. Skulick would be monitoring the CCTV feed. Technological as well as mystical security measures protected the fortress-like warehouse. Our top-of-the line electronic security system coexisted with magical wards and glyphs capable of deflecting most supernatural assaults. Should some demon locate our base of operations, the beast would have a hell of a fight if it tried to overcome our metaphysical defenses.

Like myself, Skulick wasn't a mage but had picked

up a few tricks over the years. He might not be able to cast a spell, but he knew how to draw the right protective symbols and release their power with the help of occult ritual. He'd done most of the warding himself, before his injury.

While our underground parking structure was large enough to accommodate eight vehicles, at the moment only my Ducati and Skulick's battered Humvee were parked there. The Humvee had been gathering dust for eight months. A spinal injury had a way of turning the most energetic person into a homebody.

I parked the Equus, killed the engine and got out. Stale air tinged with city grime made me immediately miss the countryside. My footsteps echoed as I approached the rusty freight elevator. I punched a button and the lift rumbled to life with a disconcerting groan of steel. Less than a minute later, the elevator door zoomed open with a metallic *thunk* and I entered the spacious loft Skulick and I called home.

The world outside the warehouse might resemble a post-apocalyptic wasteland, but the loft itself was a different story. Hardwood floors, stainless steel counters and red brick walls dominated the space. Thick beams formed an intricate web across the high ceiling, and gargantuan windows offered a perfect view of the Cursed City's glittering skyline. There was a sense of peace and tranquility within our loft, allowing us to at least momentarily forget the horrors we faced beyond these walls.

A whirring sound drew my attention and I turned to see Skulick's motorized wheelchair buzzing toward me. Behind him was a massive desk covered with computer monitors and books on the occult. Seeing Skulick, the man who became my guardian and mentor after my parents' death, brought a bittersweet smile to my face.

Growing up, I had been led to believe that my father was a traveling salesman who worked hard to support us. His business partner was John Skulick. Back then I tried to imagine what my dad's long days on the road were like. Little did I know that those trips weren't like anything my young mind imagined. It turns out that my dad and Skulick had been hunting creatures of the night, keeping the world safe from monsters.

Skulick was in his early fifties now, about the same age my father would be had he lived. A vicious scar split his ruggedly handsome features, but his warrior spirit still burned bright behind the penetrating, cunning gaze. The man had battled werewolves and vampires, wraiths and demons for decades until his broken back finally forced him from the field. He was the world's leading expert on the supernatural and, truth be told, he made me look like a rank amateur.

It pained me to see him like this, an indomitable will trapped inside a shattered body. While his injuries kept him off the front lines, he was still a driving force in the war against the forces of darkness. A thick occult tome written in some ancient language rested in his lap, a reminder that he hadn't spent these days idle while I battled a witch in the woods. He might not be able to physically engage the enemy any longer, but he could still draw on his intellect.

Skulick's lips twisted into a grin. "Welcome back, kid. Glad to see you're still in one piece."

He spun his chair toward a nearby bar and poured us two whiskeys. I gratefully accepted the tumbler. I'd been fighting the temptation of a stiff drink ever since defeating the Blackmore Witch. As the alcohol burned down my throat, my sore muscles relaxed almost immediately.

I took note of the heavy tome of occult literature propped up next to the computer terminal. The ominous title read *The Roman Manual of Demonic Magic*. Arching an eyebrow, I asked, "Catching up on some light reading?"

"Someone has to be the brains of this operation. What I learn today may save your ass tomorrow."

I chuckled and raised my glass. Couldn't argue with that logic.

"So how did it go out there, kid?" Skulick asked. He looked me over for a beat and added, "You look like hell."

"Are you trying to hurt my feelings?"

"You can always dye the gray in your hair, you know."

I scowled. "You're a real comedian."

"I have plenty of time nowadays to practice my routine."

The joke failed to mask the pain behind the words. I knew Skulick hated being trapped in this place, but he tried to make the best of it. The man was a born fighter, one of the many reasons I admired him so much. If our places were reversed, I don't think I would bear the tragic turn of events with nearly as much grace as he had.

"Kove sends his regards," I said.

"How is our old friend?"

"Country life was agreeing with him until recently."

Skulick pursed his lips. "So our hunch turned out to be right? The Blackmore Witch was responsible for these kidnappings?"

I nodded grimly. "She was turning our missing hikers into her personal gardening project. Nasty piece of business."

The humor seeped from Skulick's eyes. "Any survivors?"

I closed my eyes briefly. "Just one," I said, and raised my arm to knock back the rest of my drink. Skulick's hand snapped out, closing around my wrist. His eyes burned with a sharp intensity as he spoke. "I know what's going through your mind, kid, but there was nothing you could've done to help those poor souls. The witch did this. You aren't responsible."

"Tell that to them," I said. "Every time I close my eyes, I see the faces from those missing person posters."

"The dead are gone," Skulick said. "You have to let them go."

We were getting close to dangerous territory. Skulick knew that I felt guilty for being alive when my parents perished two decades earlier.

"Think of all the lives you saved," he continued. "If you hadn't put a stop to her, the witch would have kept killing."

On a rational level, I knew Skulick was right, but my emotions resisted his words. My partner understood me better than anybody. Skulick had arrived too late to save my parents. The guilt consumed him for years too, until he finally let it go. We both felt that we'd failed my father, and in our own ways, I think we were still trying to atone for it.

"How did you defeat her? I know how challenging spell-slingers can be."

I removed a few shards of the broken cauldron from my satchel and handed them to Skulick. He inspected the pieces with grave interest and when he was done, let out a low whistle of appreciation. He looked up at me with shining eyes. The study of new relics always made him look like an overgrown kid on Christmas Eve.

"The cauldron of the Warlock Methusan, unless I'm mistaken. The common belief among historians is that the Knights Templar destroyed the relic back in the Middle Ages."

"Looks like the historians got that one wrong," I said. "I saw a vision when I touched it. A few kids who didn't know better accidentally activated the evil thing after it lay dormant for all these decades. What are the chances of that?"

Skulick pursed his lips and shot me a knowing look. "Hell favors fools. The forces of darkness take advantage of our ignorance."

I know what he meant. The twenty-first century worshipped science, not magic. Unfortunately, our progress came at a steep price. In our haste to master the laws of nature, mankind had sacrificed its hard-earned knowledge of the mystical world. Ancient wisdom was scoffed at, reduced in people's minds to nothing but a bunch of superstitious nonsense. Modern man refused to acknowledge what science failed to explain, and the agents of darkness were more than willing to exploit our blind spot.

"You better secure these pieces," Skulick said. "There might be latent traces of power here."

I nodded. The mark of the demon on my chest had been mildly irritated during my drive back, giving credence to Skulick's concerns. The broken relic still posed a potential threat.

"I'll take care of it right now."

With these words, I turned away from my mentor and headed for the spiral staircase that led to the warehouse's top floor. Upstairs, a massive steel door inscribed with wards greeted me. The vault-like chamber behind the door contained a vast collection of the most dangerous magical relics known to mankind. We used the vault to secure black magic items that we'd come across over the years. Only once the remnants of the cauldron were safely locked away would I be able to fully relax.

I tapped a secret code into a keypad and the magic-protected steel door rumbled open. I stepped inside the windowless chamber, which was reinforced by silver. The room felt like a museum with its occult relics neatly lined up on a variety of tables and shelves. The items hummed with a seductive, evil energy.

It took a certain amount of mental discipline to be in this room for more than a few minutes. The cursed collection called out to me, a steady, incessant whisper urging me to remove them from the chamber. It had taken years of apprenticeship under Skulick's careful guidance before he allowed me to set foot inside the vault. I had to earn the right to handle these dangerous relics.

Tapping into my training, I blocked out the various voices pulling at my thoughts like a chorus of the damned and placed the shards of the cauldron on one of the empty shelves.

My task complete, I cut a hasty retreat. As the blast-resistant door slammed shut behind me, I let out a sigh of relief. The concentrated evil trapped within the chamber's walls made my skin crawl and stomach tighten up with existential terror. No wonder Skulick had nicknamed the vault "The Waiting Room to Hell."

I returned to the living area, where Skulick now faced his bank of computer monitors and big-screen TVs. The heart of our command center was his personal window to the world.

I glanced at the screens. "Anything happening that I should be aware of?"

"You could say that. We have a new client."

Skulick tapped a key, and a picture of a striking young woman appeared onscreen. She wore black lipstick and eyeliner, her hair dyed blue and styled in a mohawk. Both her upper lip and nose were pierced, heightening her sense of dangerous sexuality and punk rock disaffection. She looked like trouble.

"Who is she?" I asked.

"Meet Celeste Solos."

I took a step toward the computers and leaned forward, studying her face.

"Your type?" Skulick asked with a grin.

I shook my head a little too quickly and said, "You know me. I like nice girls. Nurses, accountants."

"Accountants don't date men who hunt demons for a living."

The man had a point. This life wasn't for anyone who cherished stability and normalcy. I came with a ton of baggage.

"I'm not interested, anyway," I snapped. "I see enough weird shit out there without going on a date with some wannabe demon groupie."

Skulick leveled his gaze at me. "Considering your chosen line of work, kid, you shouldn't be so judgmental. For all you know, this girl is a perfect angel. And regardless, she's our client."

I sighed. The woman onscreen sure didn't look like an angel. Well, maybe a fallen angel. Most of my relationships were of the one-night variety, and girls like Celeste were the ones I tended to end up with after a long night of knocking back shots at the local dive bar. They were fun and they didn't seem to mind my pentagram ring, vintage muscle car and lack of a traditional corporate job.

Hunting monsters just wasn't compatible with romance, and over the years I'd come to accept that a real relationship wasn't in the cards for me. I wasn't exactly the type of guy to settle down and start a family. It wouldn't be fair to them. As a result, I'd become pretty good at avoiding women with any serious long-term potential.

Skulick worried about my lone wolf lifestyle despite being guilty of it himself. Talk about the pot calling the kettle black. I guess in Skulick's mind, he'd at least had a real life up until his early thirties, before tragedy set him on his current path. A vampire turned his fiancée into a creature of the night, transforming the former homicide detective into a professional monster hunter.

I'd never had a chance. When most young men were dating and falling in love for the first time, I was battling monsters that wanted to wear my face and devour my soul.

Eager to get back to the business at hand, I stopped weighing the challenges of my personal life and said, "Tell me about the case. What's her problem?"

"Two words: daddy issues."

This statement earned Skulick a long look from me. "Seriously?"

"Her father sold her soul to a demon on the day she was born. And Hell is getting ready to collect their prize."

Damn. Talk about a dysfunctional family.

I opted for the only sane response when you know you're about to pick a fight with a demon. I stepped up to our bar, poured myself another shot of whiskey, and knocked it back in one quick swig.

The alcohol sizzled down my throat again but this time, it failed to calm my ragged nerves.

5

I was on my way to meet with Celeste Solos. Skulick had told Celeste to come to Aroma Mocha, a trendy coffee house in the heart of the city that doubled as our conference room when meeting potential clients. Aiming to be bohemian, mom-and-pop counter programming to Starbucks, the shop served up affordable fare in an artsy, chill environment.

The delicious smell of roasting beans and a faint whiff of butter greeted my senses. Hunting demons burned its fair share of calories, and my stomach was growling. I ordered a bagel loaded with cream cheese and an Americano.

Carbs and caffeine in hand, I settled in at a table in the corner of the shop. A surreal painting by some local artist looked down on me as I waited.

There was no sign of Celeste, but I'd arrived about

fifteen minutes before our scheduled appointment. I used the extra time to indulge in one of my other favorite pastimes—people watching.

The coffee shop attracted customers from all walks of life. Bearded hipsters and girls in steampunk finery rubbed elbows with professionals in sharp business suits. For a moment I wondered what their lives might be like. What would it be like to have a normal job, a normal life? How did it feel to not have to worry about demons and monsters on a daily basis?

My musings came to an abrupt halt when my client walked through the door. Every man—and a few of the women—perked up as she entered the coffee shop. There was a defiant quality about her beauty that made people take notice. Her attempt at downplaying her sex appeal only enhanced it.

Celeste's eyes combed the shop and spotted me. There was a flicker of a smile as she strode toward me. As in her photo, her makeup was extravagant, yet artfully applied. However, the purple eyeliner and fiery red lipstick failed to mask her haunted expression.

"Mr. Raven?"

I nodded and offered her my hand.

"It's nice to meet you, Ms. Solos."

"Please, call me Celeste."

"Hi, Celeste. Would you like me to get you a cup of coffee? Or maybe something to munch on?"

"Thank you, but that won't be necessary. I've been up for days, and I'm pretty jittery as is. Coffee might push me over the edge."

As Celeste took a seat, I noticed that her makeup couldn't quite conceal the heavy bags under her eyes. Knowing that you were about to spend eternity in Hell had a way of messing with one's sleep cycle. The piercings, the leather jacket, the combat boots—they were all part of her armor, an illusion of strength meant to distract from the scared young woman now seated across from me. I opted for some small talk to begin the meeting. Frankly, I was worried that if I pushed this girl too hard, she would bolt.

"How did you find out about what we do? We don't exactly advertise."

"Mr. Raven, once I became aware of my particular problem, I started looking into my options. You and your partner have developed a bit of a reputation around these parts."

Celeste was referring to a number of recent, high-profile occult murder cases, which the press had followed with sensationalistic glee. A number of these stories mentioned my role as a special consultant.

Most of the mundane world viewed people like me

as charlatans who wasted time and taxpayer money by claiming to have insight into the paranormal. Even though some of the articles acknowledged the rise of strange cases in our city, none considered the possibility that genuine demonic forces might be at work. Somehow Celeste, in her desperation, had figured out that there might be more to "R & S Paranormal Investigations" than the press would lead one to believe.

The public's ignorance of the supernatural emboldened the forces of darkness, but it also made my job a lot easier. I firmly believed the city was better off without knowing the truth. The resulting panic and terror wouldn't be pretty, and even more demons would take the opportunity to feed off the city's fear. Better for society to keep clinging to its comforting illusions. Celeste fiddled with one of her piercings. "Just out of curiosity, do you get a lot of cases like mine?"

"Each case is different," I said. I was telling the truth. The imagination of our enemies seemed without limits.

"How did you-"

"Let's talk about your situation," I said firmly. I didn't want this meeting to become about me. "My partner told me about it, but it would be better if you tell me everything from the beginning. How did you discover-"

"That my immortal soul was on its way to Hell?" Her

smile vanished. "It all started when I decided to find my real father."

I took a sip from my Americano and nodded. "Go on."

"I was raised to believe that my father had abandoned my mother when I was born. Which in a sense was true. Over the years, whenever I'd ask my mom who my father was, she'd go silent. Six months ago, I started having these vivid, horrific dreams; visions of demons dragging me into the burning rivers of Hell. At first I tried to keep it to myself. I've always had an overactive imagination and felt drawn to the weird and the strange. But these nightmares were different. They felt real."

That's because they're more like movie trailers than dreams, I thought grimly. *Demons love to give their victims a preview of what's to come.*

It was all beginning to add up. The date on which the demon planned to collect its price was approaching fast. Even as we spoke, the forces of darkness were gathering around Celeste in hungry anticipation.

"I still live with my mother, and she could tell I was having problems sleeping. When I opened up to her about my dreams, she came clean."

Celeste chewed on her lip for a moment before continuing. "In my dreams I'm always strapped to an altar, and I can see a tall, bald man with a beard looking down on me. When I described this man to my mother, she showed me this."

Celeste extricated a folded newspaper article from her studded leather jacket. I scanned the headline: DESMOND HORNE'S MEDIA EMPIRE EXPANDS. The man matched Celeste's description to a T. The long beard, thick eyebrows and bald head all contributed to the man's magnetic presence. He had to be in his mid-sixties now, his skin lined with wrinkles. Nevertheless, age had failed to temper the iron will smoldering in those eyes. There was a pugnacious confidence in his ascetic features that must've served him well in the business world.

"The man you're looking at is my father. Desmond Horne, one of the richest, most influential men in the city."

Horne was a celebrity of sorts, having appeared on the news on numerous occasions over the years. He was the CEO of one of the world's biggest media conglomerates, which included publishing companies, newspapers, television networks and even a movie studio.

Celeste was struggling to keep it together. Telling me her story was like opening up an old wound. "My mother was Horne's housekeeper a little over twenty years ago, and he brought her under his spell. Even though Horne was married with three children, my mother gave herself to him and got pregnant." Celeste broke off, tears threatening to overwhelm her again. She took a deep breath and continued, "All my life I believed that my father was some loser who dumped us. The truth was different. He paid my mother to raise me on her own. Every year, she received a check with a lot of zeroes on it, in exchange for keeping her mouth shut."

"I'm sorry," I said because it seemed like the right thing to say. She acknowledged my words with a thin smile.

"Horne targeted my mom because he needed someone new to this country, someone who wouldn't make waves, someone who would accept a payoff."

"Your mother must have been in the dark about Horne's bargain."

"Yes, thank God."

I raised an eyebrow and asked, "Then how did you figure out the rest?"

"After I learned about Horne being my father, I tried to contact him. He steadfastly refused to return my emails and calls. I finally showed up one day at his mansion. His security forces tried to send me away, but his wife stopped them. She was the one who finally broke down and told me the rest of the story. There's a temple in their mansion where Horne does... unspeakable things. She told me about the ritual my father used me in, twenty years ago. The guilt had consumed her for years."

Her hands balled into fists, lips pressed into a thin line. "I did some more digging after that. Two decades ago, Desmond Horne was a reasonably successful businessman, but his career took off big-time after I was born. Now I know why."

Tears gave way to anger as she added, "My father knocked up my mom so he could trade his own flesh and blood for money and power."

It all made sense. Desmond Horne's formidable business success was attributable to a demon's help. The soul of an innocent child was valuable currency in Hell. Who cared if the bastard child of some poor, immigrant housekeeper ended up becoming collateral damage?

I did, for a start. And so did Skulick.

Celeste pulled up the arm of her leather jacket and revealed a fiery red scar not unlike the one on my chest. It was the signature of a demon. The beast had marked his future property when she was only an infant.

"After I found out about my father and the cult, I hit the library. Tried to read as many books on demons as I could get my hands on. I wanted to know everything, but especially why my father didn't just sacrifice me on the day I was born."

I knew the answer to this question. "Hell wants a

fully formed soul. A soul with dreams, hopes, aspirations."

Demons feed off anger, fear and despair. What disappointment could be greater than having a life cut down in its prime?

Tears welled up in Celeste's eyes and I found myself reaching out and squeezing her hand. She tried to wipe the tears away and ended up smudging her makeup.

The cruelty of the situation was overwhelming. Losing my parents had been terrible, but at least I knew they died protecting me. In Celeste's case, the people who were supposed to keep her safe were the ones who'd sold her out. That was a rough place to come back from.

"How much longer do I have?" Celeste asked, her voice drained of emotion. I wasn't an expert when it came to the rules that governed Faustian pacts, but if Celeste's dreams and visions were any indicator, her time would soon be up.

"It depends on the ritual, but generally Hell collects souls on a milestone birthday. Eighteen is a popular one."

Celeste's face turned a ghastly white. "My twenty-first birthday is in two days."

My fingers tightened around the arms of my chair. This meant we had less than twenty-four hours to undo what had been done to this young woman. Finding a way to break such an infernal pact would have been difficult enough, but doing it in less than 48 hours was, well, impossible.

"It's too late, isn't it?" Celeste said, reading my expression.

I thought about giving her false hope, but Celeste deserved to know what she was up against.

"I'm sorry," I said again, and this time I meant it from the depths of my own weary soul.

I was still trying to figure out our next move when outside forces made the choice for me. I hadn't paid much attention to the homeless man enthusiastically rummaging through a large, full trashcan facing the coffee shop's window. Such a sight is, sadly, increasingly common in the city.

I started paying attention when the man suddenly turned toward us, an eerie scarecrow outlined by the mist that was rapidly gathering on the street. Scavenger hunt suddenly forgotten, the homeless man's posture changed. His body grew rigid while his eyes narrowed into menacing slits.

Celeste must've picked up on my interest, and she followed my gaze. That's when the homeless man's grimy fingers gripped the trashcan and lifted it into the air with nearly superhuman strength. For a beat he just stood there, the thing raised high above his head like some stinking trophy. He grinned—a nightmarish sight with his mouth of yellowed teeth—and heaved the can toward us. A second later, the storefront window of Aroma Mocha shattered into a thousand pieces.

6

I reacted with the speed of someone used to sudden, violent attacks. One moment I was sipping my Americano and the next I was pulling my new client from the path of the oncoming trashcan. One arm raised, I relied on my coat to shield us from the hail of glass as we both slammed to the floor. The metal canister had to weigh at least sixty pounds and our table splintered under the teeth-chattering impact. Can, table, glassware and trash hit the ground a split second later, causing a colossal din.

A quick survey of the shop revealed a crowd of stunned onlookers. Baristas stood frozen in place, lattes and cappuccinos momentarily forgotten.

I stumbled to my feet, pulling Celeste along with me, just as the homeless man stomped through the shattered display window, murder in his eyes. Our assailant projected an air of deranged menace. He moved with a speed and strength that belied his emaciated frame. He was not, in fact, a man at all anymore, but a puppet under the control of evil.

Most demons navigate our world inside human hosts. Physical manifestation is possible but far more rare because it requires a great expenditure of energy. This ruled out using *Hellseeker* against our attacker. The hapless man before me was as much of a victim as Celeste. Demons exploited the weak-minded and mentally deranged, taking advantage of lost individuals easily swayed and seduced by their terrible lies and empty promises.

The homeless man's eyes burned with demonic fury as he launched himself at me. I darted aside and he sailed past me, missing by inches. He crumpled against the counter, knocking over an expensive-looking espresso machine. Damn it all. No matter how things ended here today, I was going to have to find a new coffee shop. I really liked this place, too.

Our possessed attacker shook his head with a grunt and scrambled back to his feet. He looked up just in time for me to drive my fist, empowered by the magical *Seal of Solomon* ring I wore, into his face. A spark of mystical energy flew as my fist impacted his jaw. The man fell back, moaning feebly. I spun toward a stunned

Celeste, snatched her hand and stormed toward the exit. The other patrons gazed at us as we made our rapid departure, but no one uttered a word.

Tendrils of heavy mist enveloped us as we emerged from the coffee shop. The nearby demon was manipulating weather conditions. Even though I had defeated its human puppet, we were far from being safe. First order of business was for us to get to my car, which was parked at the end of the block. The Equus Bass' protective wards would hold off any future demonic attacks. Or at least I hoped they would. I could decide on our next move once we reached the car.

With this purpose driving me, I rushed down the block. Celeste was following my lead, not asking questions or slowing me down with hysterics. When I glanced over my shoulder at her, she was wearing an expression of fierce determination. Between that, the piercings and the mohawk, she looked like some kind of barbarian warrior queen.

I stumbled to a halt as a tall man wearing a thousand-dollar suit and a shiny Rolex peeled from the fog ahead of us, blocking our advance. The man's eyes turned crimson and a forked tongue flickered from his mouth. Great. Another civilian under the command of a demonic force. Had the original beast found a new host, or was a second demon joining the fray?

Either way, this lawyer from hell meant business. With a ferocious roar, he whipped his briefcase at us. I dodged the first attack and tackled the possessed man before he could go on the offensive again. We both slammed into the nearest parked car, the passenger side window spider-webbing on impact.

The man let out a surprised moan and I pulled away from him. He blinked and looked up at me with ordinary—albeit confused—brown eyes.

"What happened?" he said.

"Watch out!" Celeste screamed.

The warning came a second too late as a pair of massive hands wrapped themselves around my throat. I faced my attacker, trying feebly to loosen the vise-like hold. The demon had switched bodies again. He now wore the thickly muscled form of a construction worker. I gasped for air as stars danced before my eyes.

"Her soul belongs to us, Raven!" the demon inside the construction worker hissed. Us? Could this be the demon Celeste's soul was promised to?

Doubt it.

A full-fledged demon would only materialize on the day his victim's soul was due. Showing up earlier would be beneath such a creature. Still, that wouldn't stop him from sending lesser demons, known as *hellhounds*, after his prey in the hours leading up to that fateful moment.

These messengers couldn't collect the prize directly, but their presence would heighten the despair of the target.

"Stay out of this or pay the ultimate—"

The words died on the hellhound's lips as my protective ring came up into his face. My attacker exhaled sharply and the grip around my neck loosened. A moment later, Celeste and I were storming toward my Equus Bass 770.

Once my new client was safely inside the car I got behind the wheel, massaging my bruised throat. The second I slammed the door shut the construction worker reappeared, pissed as all hell. The massive man hurled his bulk against the windshield and the wards lit up like the Las Vegas Strip. Blue energy crackled as the car's protective magic tossed our new friend aside. The man went flying and disappeared into the mist.

I hadn't even turned the key in the ignition when he was replaced by an armed police officer. The cop's eyes flashed red as he leveled his pistol at my windshield. The wards worked great against paranormal attacks, but didn't fare quite as well against bullets. The demon must've evacuated the previous host before he even hit the ground.

Clever beast.

A bullet blew my right-hand wing mirror away in a

hail of sparking metal and glass. I took this as my cue to fire up the engine and get the hell out of there.

I heard more cracks of gunfire, but luckily the projectiles kept hitting metal instead of flesh. Fog devoured the possessed officer as he receded in my rear-view mirror.

Yes! We made it! Score one for the agents of light.

My elation proved short-lived. As we hurtled down the foggy block, I cut a sharp right and...

...found myself back in front of the coffee house.

The cop stood before us, loading a fresh magazine into his pistol.

Shit, this wasn't going to be pretty.

"What's going on? Oh my God, it's like we never left!"

I shut out Celeste's panicky voice and turned inward. Losing my cool at this critical juncture wouldn't help anyone.

Despite their considerable powers, there were rules demons had to play by while on our earthly plane. Distorting or reshaping reality was possible, but it would require an enormous amount of energy. Celeste's soul was precious, but I found it hard to believe hell-hounds could push reality to such a degree. I had managed to cover an entire city block before we were looped back here. To pull off such a feat would require an unimaginable amount of power.

A realization hit me; the demon hadn't distorted physical reality, only our perception of it. This was a demonic mind trick, nothing more. Which meant we were still on the road.

The sudden insight shattered the demonic illusion. All this time we'd been in motion, my Equus Bass 770 roaring along at full speed. As reality snapped back to normal, I saw that the Equus Bass had veered into the path of an oncoming bus. I recognized the terror in the bus driver's eyes—it mirrored my own.

Celeste let out a shrill scream as I twisted the steering wheel and cut back into my lane. The bus barreled past and almost clipped us as the tortured wail of screeching tires filled the air. A cold sweat ran down my face. Had I failed to snap out of the illusion, Celeste and I would now be wrapped in a cocoon of twisted metal and shattered glass. Not exactly a comforting visual.

I turned toward Celeste, who stared at me with shocked eyes. "What just happened?"

The demon almost won, I thought, but I kept my mouth shut. As the road flashed by, another realization sunk in. The mark of the demon on my chest hadn't lit up during the attack. Talk about disturbing developments. I relied on my scar to detect approaching threats; it had saved my ass on numerous occasions and prevented the creatures of the night from catching me off guard. So why had it failed me today?

"I'm sorry," Celeste said, breaking my chain of thought.

Her voice quaked as she continued, "Meeting me put you in terrible danger. I should never have gotten you involved."

"Listen, Celeste, this is what I do. I fight the dark side. I eat demons for breakfast."

I grinned, but she didn't seem convinced by my bravado. Her eyes were dull with defeat. If she succumbed to despair, the demon would win.

"How can one hope to beat the devil himself?" she muttered.

Excellent question. Skulick and I had been trying to answer it for the last few years, ever since the door between our realms was cracked open. We weren't any closer to figuring it out. All I knew was that I had to stand up to a bully, no matter how powerful he might be.

"I need to buy us some time," I said. "Learn more about the demon. The more we know about the enemy we're up against here, the better our odds…"

Of saving your soul, I thought, but kept that last part to myself. Celeste was all too aware of the stakes without me having to remind her again. Instead I tried to say something a bit more encouraging. "My partner has forgotten more about demonology than I'll ever know. He might have some ideas."

Skulick wouldn't approve of what I was about to do next, but I didn't see any other choice. I turned left and jumped onto the freeway. My new destination was the one place in this city that was off limits to Hell's infernal legions.

7

L ook up "inner sanctum" in the dictionary and you'll get the following definition: *A private or secret place to which few other people are admitted to.* I was bringing Celeste to our own secret place and breaking one of our key rules of engagement. Our headquarters was off-limits to clients. But I couldn't just leave her out in the cold.

Celeste's situation was different from our usual cases. The way I saw it, I didn't have much of a choice. Nevertheless, I expected Skulick to be pissed.

I turned out to be right.

My partner was waiting for us at the elevator, and his disapproving scowl spoke volumes. Before I could explain myself, he brusquely pulled me aside. His legs might be useless, but his upper body rippled with muscle. "Ms. Solos, it's a pleasure meeting you in person," he said, putting emphasis on the last two words, "but would you please excuse me for a moment while I have a quick word with my partner? We'll be right with you."

We were barely out of hearing range when Skulick got into it. "What were you thinking, bringing her here?"

"There's no other way. We were attacked by hellhounds!"

"And now they have her scent. She'll lead them right to us."

"I couldn't hold off a sustained demonic assault out there on my own. At least here, we stand a fighting chance. The wards will hold them back."

"Can you be certain of that? We don't even know which entity we're up against."

"That's your department," I retorted, unable to suppress my own growing irritation. "I thought this through, believe me."

Skulick stole another mistrustful glance at Celeste, who leaned uncertainly against the elevator door. "Which head were you doing your thinking with?"

Most paranormal investigators died relatively young. It was part of the gig. A highly developed sense of paranoia accounted for Skulick's long tour of duty in the war against the darkness. From his perspective, bringing the doomed girl here probably ranked among the dumbest things I'd ever done—and keep in mind that this man raised me during my teenage years. But I remained convinced that I'd made the right choice. Bringing Celeste to our loft would buy us enough time to plan an effective countermove before the next attack.

Celeste wiped tears from her face, struggling to keep it together. Skulick softened. My partner can be tough as nails, but underneath the steel there does beat a warm, deeply caring heart. He's basically a big softie, when you get down to it. None of those gentler feelings were reserved for me at the moment. He shot me a final glare for good measure before his wheelchair buzzed toward our guest.

Wheeling up to Celeste, he cranked up the charm, his scowl miraculously stretching into a reassuring smile. "I apologize for keeping you waiting." Skulick nodded at a sleek leather couch. "Please take a seat. Is there something we can offer you to drink?"

A shaken Celeste glanced longingly at our fully stocked bar.

"Anything with alcohol will do."

Skulick's smile deepened. He shot me a quick look and said, "Be a gentleman and get the lady a drink, would ya?"

I obliged while Skulick began to interview our client. I hated petty arguments, and I was glad to see my partner directing his considerable intellect toward the problem at hand.

"We'll need to find out more about the particular demon we're up against," Skulick said to Celeste. "You can help us by telling me everything you know about this cult your father was involved in."

"I wish I could be of more help," Celeste said, "but up until a few weeks ago I didn't even know who my father was."

Skulick studied her with a thoughtful expression before turning toward his bank of monitors. He tapped a few keys and Desmond Horne's image filled the large flat-screen TV facing the room.

"Reviewing your father's meteoric success over the last twenty-one years might point us in the right direction. Selling your soul was clearly a business transaction, and one that gave him considerable rewards."

I scratched my jaw thoughtfully. "Think we're dealing with Mammon, the demon of wealth and greed?"

"It's a possibility," Skulick said. "But there are other, less powerful entities out there who might offer financial gains in exchange for an innocent soul."

I finished pouring drinks—one for Celeste, and one for me. She took her whiskey with a grateful smile and downed it in one gulp. I liked a woman who could hold her liquor.

"You mentioned on the phone that you were suffering from nightmares," Skulick continued. "Maybe you can tell us more about your dreams. They could provide further clues as to the identity of this entity."

"I'll tell you everything I know," she said, holding up her empty glass to show me that a refill would not be unwelcome.

"Before we continue, there's something we should do. The demon's hellhounds have caught your scent and won't rest until they find you. They'll be able to track you no matter where you hide. The wards will throw them off your trail for a little bit, but they'll locate you soon enough. There might be a way to delay them, however."

I frowned, curious. Skulick continued, "One of the most effective charms against evil is the Prayer to St. Michael. Even better, though—"

"Is the Medal of the Saints, also known as the armor of God," I finished.

A year earlier, Skulick and I had traveled to Slovakia to investigate reports of mass possession. A local priest, Father Jozef Horvath, assisted us in our battle and offered up the Christian relic in thanks. It had played an essential role in the successful outcome of the case, and now we kept it under tight lock and key inside the vault upstairs. Not only did the vault safeguard evil relics, it also acted as a storage space for potent talismans we were saving for a rainy day.

A day like today.

If Celeste wore the Medal of the Saints around her neck, she would become invisible to the demonic blood-hounds looking for her. At least for a short while.

"I'll get the medal right now," I volunteered.

Skulick nodded and for the second time in the last twenty-four hours, I climbed the winding staircase leading up to the vault. There was a bounce in my step this time. For a change I wasn't locking away a cursed object but retrieving a blessed item that would help us protect an innocent woman.

As I waited impatiently for the vault door to swing open, I mulled over the facts of this unusual case. Skulick had a point—there were a number of other enti-ties Horne might have bargained with besides Mammon. Cromeck, with his power over goods and money, came to mind. Or perhaps Atlonioa, whose sphere of influence included finance and wealth.

The list went on. Skulick was the real expert when it came to demonology. I'd picked up a few things over the years, but if anyone could hope to identify the demonic entity hunting Celeste, it was my partner.

The vault opened and I stepped inside. It took me less than a minute to locate the Medal of the Saints. The round amulet was cast from silver, and a crucifix adorned its surface surrounded by a series of letters: C.S.S.M.L. They stood for *Crux Sacra Sit Mihi Lux,* a Latin phrase meaning "May the Holy Cross Be for Me a Light."

As soon as I touched the pendant, the shrill voices around me faded out and I experienced a deep sense of calm. The power of the amulet was considerable, and I felt hopeful that it would keep Celeste safe for a while.

I was about to leave the vault when a sound to my left gave me pause. I was used to hearing insidious whispers within these silver-reinforced walls, but this sounded more like approaching footsteps. A chill tore up my spine. Someone else had entered the vault. I spun around and came face to face with our client. I hesitated... and this turned out to be a terrible mistake.

"Celeste?"

Her answer was to raise her arm and point a taser right at my chest.

She pulled the trigger without hesitation and fifty thousand volts of electricity zapped me.

I went down face first, hitting the ground in a mass of excruciating muscle contractions. Nerves on fire, I couldn't concentrate on anything but the pain surging through my body.

Celeste knelt next to me and scooped up the pendant from the floor near my twitching form. She then turned to one of the many shelves inside the vault.

Celeste was after more than the Medal of Saints.

She removed another relic from one of the shelves. In her hand, she held an ancient dagger. The knife's main blade was flanked by two smaller ones, similar to a Japanese sai. I struggled to remember the occult significance of the three-pronged knife.

Most of the items in the vault remained shrouded in mystery. Even though I'd known Skulick for more than two decades, we'd only hunted monsters together for the last six years. Skulick had refused to let me engage in field work until I left him no choice in the matter. For the most part, the collection represented Skulick's life's work, the sum total of his years battling the dark side. I wasn't privy to the exact magical properties of most of these items, but I knew that Skulick had a pretty damn good reason for keeping them all sealed inside this chamber.

As Celeste leaned over me, the magical nature of the blade in her hand ceased to be my biggest worry. The razor-sharp dagger could cause plenty of damage on its own. I willed myself to move, but my muscles remained uncooperative.

To my surprise, Celeste used the dagger to draw a line on the palm of her hand. She leaned closer and allowed her warm blood to drip over my face. I tasted copper and my stomach clenched with revulsion.

"I'm sorry, Raven. There's no other way."

With these words she rose and turned away. Seconds later, she vanished through the open vault door. My body was on fire, but the pain paled in comparison with the cold sense of betrayal I felt.

Celeste had played us all.

8

L ying sprawled on the vault floor, the feeling of betrayal gave way to another emotion—concern for my partner. Despite being wheel-chair-bound, Skulick wouldn't have allowed Celeste to access the top floor without a fight. He could be a real pain at times, but he was the closest thing to family in my life. The thought of him being hurt—or worse—drove an icy wedge of terror into my heart.

I had to get back to my feet. Unfortunately, my body refused to cooperate. Damn, how could I've been so foolish? I had allowed a complete stranger into our base. Who knew what else Celeste might be up to? Was she working in collusion with the demon?

The thought sent another wave of cold fear through my paralyzed form. I fought back visions of Celeste disabling the wards and allowing our greatest enemies access to the loft. Maybe the theft of the dagger only served as a prelude to a far greater plan of attack. In the worst-case scenario, Skulick and I would end up dead and the treasure trove of mystical objects we protected would fall into the hands of the very creatures we had vowed to defeat.

Frustration building, I attempted to move again and this time my fingers wiggled as my stunned muscles finally remembered who was supposed to be in charge here. My limbs still felt like bags of cement as, after ten minutes of gradual improvement, I was able to stand again.

One excruciating step at a time, I made my way out of the vault. The loft felt eerily quiet and my concern for my partner's wellbeing grew with each step. I eyed the staircase before me and figured the elevator was the better option; considering my current state, I'd probably fall down the stairs and break my legs.

It would serve you right, I thought.

"Skulick? You okay?" I croaked.

Silence.

Even if Skulick *was* all right, he probably couldn't hear me from all the way up here. I stumbled toward the elevator and waited. The lift took forever to arrive. Or at least it seemed that way.

Once the doors split open to reveal the floor below,

my eyes combed our living area. They found my partner's motorized wheelchair with Skulick slumped in it,
unconscious.

I rushed over and shook his prone body, checking
for any visible injuries. There was no sign of trauma, so I
let out a sigh of relief. I hadn't experienced such panic
since the day Skulick broke his back.

"Hey, old buddy, talk to me. You okay?"

My partner's eyes fluttered open, and he regarded
me for a disoriented beat. Reality was slowly slipping
back into focus for my old friend.

"What happened?" I asked.

"Good question," Skulick said, still groggy and
blinking away the cobwebs. "One moment Celeste's
telling me about growing up without a father, the next
I'm out for the count. There was no physical violence..."

Skulick's voice trailed off, the implication clear.

"Magic," I said.

"Celeste used a low-level sleeping spell to knock me
out, as far as I can gather," Skulick said.

"Are you saying our client is a spell slinger?" I asked,
my surprise growing.

"It appears that way," Skulick said.

I couldn't quite wrap my head around the idea of
Celeste using magic.

"Why would she taze me..."

As soon as I asked the question, the answer hit me. "Celeste must've known about my protective ring. This was all one big setup."

Skulick's features filled with grim understanding. "She stole something from the vault, didn't she?"

I nodded.

"Besides the Medal of the Saints, she helped herself to a dagger. And she marked me with some of her blood, too."

Skulick's mind churned behind those intense eyes, processing this new information. I was still playing catch up here, but the pieces seemed to be coming together for him.

"What the hell is going on here?" I asked.

Somehow I knew I wouldn't be happy with the answer.

NEITHER SKULICK nor I got much sleep that night. While my partner combed through obscure texts and occult databases, I was left with the fun job of securing the warehouse. First order of business was to wash Celeste's blood from my face. Next up was making sure all our wards and surveillance systems remained in perfect working order.

We'd done an excellent job securing the facility, but the wards were designed to stop agents of darkness, not human thieves. Especially not when I invited them inside. Our own carelessness and softhearted approach to the case had enabled this fiasco. I was furious at myself.

Inspecting the garage soured my mood further. The Ducati was missing. Once I assured myself that Celeste hadn't done any more damage, I returned to the loft's main floor.

Only now that the morning sunlight slashed through the warehouse's oversized windows did sleep threaten to overwhelm me. I let out a yawn and fought the temptation to close my eyes.

I held no illusions about getting any rest today. As long as Celeste was at large with the stolen dagger, I couldn't afford to sleep. Resigning myself to a long day, I brewed a pot of strong coffee and poured two cups, one for myself and one for Skulick, whose attention remained glued to his bank of monitors and books.

I approached my partner's desk, steaming mugs in hand, and offered him a cup. Skulick didn't avert his gaze from the thick tome he was leafing through as he accepted the fiery hot brew. When Skulick tackled a problem, he did so with the ferocious, single-minded tenacity of a terrier. I blew on my coffee and hazarded a sip. "Any luck?"

"Perhaps. Take a look at our surveillance footage."

Onscreen, I watched myself pulling into the underground garage, getting out of the Equus Bass with Celeste, and then heading for the elevators. At first, there was nothing out of the ordinary about the footage. That all changed when the camera zoomed in on Celeste's face. The closer view revealed features that appeared blurred and distorted.

"What does it mean?" I asked, leaning closer to the screen.

"It means our thief was telling us the truth, at least to a degree. The electronic distortion of her image suggests that a dark force was targeting her."

In other words, her soul was indeed hellbound. That much hadn't been a lie.

"Okay, so why turn on us? And what about the dagger?"

"It's called the Soul Dagger. Used by the Berlin Ripper, a serial killer, occultist and amateur mage. Your father and I managed to bring his reign of terror to an end in the early '90s."

Good old dad, I thought. How many monsters had he and Skulick dispatched while I was growing up? Too many to count. The man had been a real hero, and Skulick and I were the only two people in the whole goddamn world who knew his story. I wished I'd known the man better.

"What's the magical significance of this dagger?" I asked.

"The name says it all. It absorbs and traps the souls of its victims."

I thought this over for a moment, recalling the way Celeste let some of her own blood dribble on my face. Almost as if Skulick had read my mind, he said, "You must be wondering why she used the dagger on herself. Those drops of blood held a trace amount of her soul."

Understanding hit me. "She marked me with her life force."

Skulick nodded grimly. "The Medal of the Saints has made Celeste invisible to the hellhounds' senses. The only scent they'll be able to pick up-"

"Is the one she left on me," I finished.

"In time, the demons' minions will recognize their error. The Medal of the Saints will shield Celeste only for a short while."

"Yeah, but by the time they realize they have the wrong soul..."

There won't be enough of me left to scrape off the floor, I finished mentally.

"You sure have a way with women, kid."

"Tell me about it," I said. "No good deed goes unpunished."

"Clearly she doubted our ability to protect her and took matters into her own hands. Miss Solos was apparently much better informed about the occult than we realized. She knew about the Medal of Saints and the Soul Dagger, knew about our operation and, from the looks of it, has dabbled extensively in magic."

I processed this. The price for dabbling in the dark arts was madness and corruption. I'd seen it too many times to doubt that Celeste would end up just like the Blackmore Witch if she wasn't stopped. It was likely that the magical abilities had already begun to poison her mind.

"What's the endgame here?" I asked. "At best, marking me with her blood buys Celeste a little time. But there has to be more to it than that."

Skulick hesitated before he answered. "A Faustian pact can't be broken. Only renegotiated."

I perked up. "How so?"

"You have to offer Hell something of greater value in exchange. And what could more valuable to a demon than Celeste's soul?"

I thought it over for a moment, and the answer hit me like a sledgehammer to the head. "Multiple souls."

As if to lend weight to my words, Skulick tapped a key and the image of the stolen Soul Dagger appeared onscreen.

"The Berlin Ripper planned to murder thirteen innocents, the most saintly people he could track down. Nuns, priests, relief workers, hero cops. People whose souls were beyond the reach of the forces of darkness."

"The dagger let him offer their souls to his dark master," I said. Celeste's plan was coming into focus. She was going to use the knife to collect souls she could trade for her own. How many? It didn't really matter. Even one life would be too many. I felt bad for her. It wasn't her fault that her father was a power-hungry son of a bitch. But if she went down this path, she would deserve Hell.

"Skulick, I'm so sorry I brought her here," I said. "I don't know what I was thinking."

Skulick's grim visage softened. "You wanted to save a young woman from a fate worse than death. Your heart was in the right place, kid. If I were twenty years younger, I would've done the same. Hard to resist a damsel in distress."

Tell me about it. But Celeste had turned out to be no damsel. Far from it.

"What's our next move? How much time do we have before Hell comes knocking on our...?"

The words died on my lips as my cell chirped. A quick scan of my phone identified the incoming caller as Homicide Detective Rob Benson, our contact person in the department now that Kove had moved on. After a year that had seen a sharp rise in occult crimes, the police had grudgingly accepted that Skulick and I could be assets. Benson's call meant he was working some occult crime scene and needed my help.

As Benson explained the reason for the call, I could feel my mood darken. Five minutes later, I cut him off with a promise to immediately head over to the crime scene.

"What's troubling the good detective?" Skulick asked.

"There's been a murder. Gabriel Horne, son of Desmond, was discovered stabbed to death in his penthouse apartment. This image was found next to the body."

I held up my cell phone for Skulick. Benson had sent me a photo of the luxury apartment turned crime scene. Of greater interest than the expensive decor was the occult symbol painted on the wall. I assumed that it had been etched in the murder victim's blood. That was the way these things usually went. The symbol was identical to the mark on Celeste's arm–the brand of the demon her soul was promised to.

If the identity of the dead man hadn't been enough, the signature left behind at the crime scene told me everything I needed to know.

The Soul Dagger had found its first victim.

9

Gabriel Horne's twenty-story luxury apartment was located in one of the ritzier areas of the city. To my surprise, I got lucky and found a parking spot without much trouble. Fatigue loomed heavy and my eyes burned with the need for sleep. I felt ragged and worn out. The lack of rest, the physical stress of confronting the Blackmore Witch—not to mention being hit by fifty thousand volts—it was all catching up to me big time. Even though I wanted to crash, sleep would have to wait. Perhaps I wasn't in the right shape to brave the world, but ready or not, here I came.

There would be no rest for the wicked today.

I guzzled the last dregs of coffee from my thermos and stepped out of the car. One drawback to mainlining caffeine on a daily basis was that you build up a tolerance. Stubborn bastard that I am, I kept hoping the next cup might somehow miraculously get the job done.

A fine drizzle shrouded me as I made my way down the sidewalk, one laborious step at a time. Ever since the Crimson Circle's ritual punched a hole into reality, the weather in this city has gone to shit. We have more rain and fog than nineteenth century London. Under normal circumstances I would've found the light rain unpleasant, but I welcomed it in my current groggy state. It proved a hell of a lot more effective in clearing my head than the coffee surging through my system.

Flashing squad cars greeted me at the main entrance of Gabriel Horne's apartment building. Uniformed cops swarmed the crowded lobby and struggled to keep a throng of reporters at bay. The Horne family was a constant fixture of both the tabloids and mainstream press, so this murder story was going to make some waves. An officer I'd seen a few times, but whose name I could never remember, waved me over.

Fortunately the reporters barely paid me any attention as I navigated the gauntlet of snapping cameras. Certain articles had mentioned my name over the past year, but I'd made a concerted effort to avoid follow-up questions. Weirdly enough, the *Seal of Solomon* helped me maintain my anonymity. The few journalists who'd tracked me down would be hard pressed to describe me.

Don't ask me how, but the magical ring dulls people's memories of my appearance, and cameras have a habit of taking blurry pics around me. The ring finds ways of keeping me safe from demonic as well as more mundane dangers. Good thing too. It's difficult enough doing this job without having to worry about the media hounding you. Skulick and I liked to operate behind the scenes as much as possible. "Shadow detectives" as he likes to call us, which is as good a name as any.

Even if any of the reporters recognized me, they had bigger fish to fry at the moment. Some occult expert with questionable credentials who looked like he just rolled out of bed couldn't compete with the story of the year.

Officer Forgot-His-Name greeted me with a curt nod. "Benson is waiting for you upstairs," he said as he escorted me to the elevator.

Catching a glance at myself in the elevator door made me flinch. I was suddenly doubly grateful that nobody wanted to take my picture. I looked like shit. Run-down, sleep-deprived shit.

The elevator doors split open and erased the scary fella staring back at me.

I followed the officer into the lift, took a deep breath, and prepared myself for what awaited me on the top floor. I had a feeling it wasn't going to be pretty.

Less than a minute later, I was inside Gabriel Horne's penthouse residence. The photograph Detective Benson had sent me didn't do the place justice. Organic textures like stone, weathered wood, and glass dominated and defined the space. A stunning three-sixty view created the impression of being inside an observatory. The polished China clay floor, the artfully twisted and curled industrial lighting fixtures, and the tasteful black and white furniture all discreetly whispered that the people who lived here were obscenely wealthy.

Just inhaling the rarified air in this place could get you laid.

I vaguely recalled that Gabriel Horne had held a cushy position in one of his daddy's media companies. Nothing wrong with nepotism, but I doubted that a father willing to sell his daughter's soul to a demon did anything out of the goodness of his heart. Gabriel Horne's gig had no doubt come with strings attached. Maybe Daddy Dearest had just wanted to keep tabs on his first-born.

Detective Benson could be found, as always, at the center of an active crime scene. Tall, African-American, and somewhere north of his mid-thirties, he looked like he could have owned the penthouse, or at least been invited here for drinks once in a while. Some cops let the stress of their work eat them up; bad lifestyle choices are common. Comfort food and alcohol are much needed and often abused psychological Band-Aids for many. Throw in the long hours, the lack of exercise, and other questionable habits, and it wasn't surprising that many cops looked like crap. Benson was different. He wore a sharp designer suit that fit his athletic physique like a glove. There was an admirable sense of discipline and self-control about the man. Standing next to him in my wrinkled trench coat and tieless shirt, I couldn't help but feel like a bum.

"About time you showed your face, Raven," Benson said. "I was starting to get worried."

"Have I ever stood you up, Benson?"

Benson eyes narrowed. He doesn't really like me too much but he knows he needs me. And I know that he knows it. Ours is a complicated relationship.

"Want to bring me to speed? Who found the body?"

"The maid. She cleans the place on a daily basis," he said. "Only access to the penthouse is by private elevator or emergency stairs."

"Did you talk to the building manager yet?"

Benson nodded. "Doorman didn't see anyone coming or going. No signs of forced entry. Some of my men are in the process of reviewing the security tapes. They show a woman entering the building not long before the murder, but her face is blurred out in every shot. I bet you have some perfectly logical explanation for that one, don't you?"

I did, actually. But I doubted Benson would be too keen to hear the truth. Celeste must've used a cloaking spell, allowing her to enter and leave the building undetected. We both were camera shy in our own way.

"Where's the body?" I asked.

Instead of answering me directly, Benson said, "Detective Archer, show him the vic."

I flinched and turned toward the female detective who'd snuck up on us. Detective Jane Archer is half Puerto Rican and a quarter each of Irish and Italian. Average height and fit enough to make an American Ninja contestant envious, she had a penchant for leather jackets and a habit of wearing her curly hair short. Archer is a skilled martial artist, great shot and excellent detective capable of thinking outside the box. Like any strong woman with a badge, most of her fellow officers assume she swings for the other team.

I know from personal experience that they're wrong. Big time. But I never kiss and tell. Especially not when the lady in question could break my bones in a variety of creative ways.

"Follow me, Raven." Her voice was all business. I didn't even get a smile.

"How have you been?" I asked.

"Fabulous. By the way, there's a new invention I've heard about—you should try it sometime. It's called a shower."

"Charming as always, Detective."

That almost got a smirk, so things were looking very slightly up. "How is the ghoul fighting business?"

"The pay's shit, the nightmares keep me up at night, and there are zero fringe benefits."

She shrugged. "Sounds a lot like being a cop."

I wanted to say something else—maybe along the lines of "Sorry I snuck out of your apartment at the crack of dawn, I'm an idiot, please call me"—but the moment passed. In case you're wondering, Archer and I did hook up. Once. Copious amounts of alcohol were involved. Our partnership never quite recovered.

Archer pointed at the back of the room. I spotted a doorway, which I assumed led into the victim's bedroom. The details of the crime scene, as far as I could see, seemed tame compared to some of the other weird cases we'd worked on in the past.

"Any idea why Benson called me in on this one?

"I think the message convinced him."

I arched an eyebrow. "What message?"

"You better take a look for yourself."

That didn't sound good. Taking a deep breath and steeling myself for the worst, I brushed by a cluster of cops. Their wary, mistrustful glances followed me. You would think they'd appreciate my help—and some did. But for many of them I represented an unknown variable, and they didn't quite know what to make of me. The supernatural was terrifying to the average person, and even some of the most hardened officers on the force wished they could forget some of the shit they'd experienced in the months following the breach. I could easily imagine what went through their minds when they looked at me. What kind of guy voluntarily seeks out these nightmares? Was I some occult ambulance chaser, a deranged crackpot, or a big phony selling myself as an expert?

I blocked out their stares and entered Gabriel Horne's bedroom. It matched the luxury of the rest of the penthouse, with vast skylights offering up yet more spectacular views of the city. A forensics team was busy collecting evidence around the king-sized bed.

The demon's mark was smeared on the wall above the bed.

"Do you mind?" I said as I approached.

The forensic guy, some baby-faced kid who looked way too innocent to be spending his days studying dead bodies, quickly checked with Archer. The detective nodded her okay, and the kid stepped aside, allowing me closer access to Gabriel. The man was only wearing a pair of blue boxers and it appeared Celeste must've killed him in his sleep. I still couldn't imagine the girl I met in the coffee shop the other day committing a violent crime like this.

I leaned over the bed and studied the wound on the man's chest. He'd been stabbed in the heart. Two smaller punctures flanked a larger gash and left no doubt as to the murder weapon. The three-pronged Soul Dagger had claimed Gabriel Horne's life.

And his soul.

"Take a look at the eyes," another member of the forensic team urged me. "Never seen anything like it."

I traded a look with Archer. We'd been hearing that phrase a lot lately.

I inched closer to the bed and looked down. Blank white orbs stared back at me. The eyes are the windows to the soul, and the magical knife had drained the man of his essence, pupil and iris veiled by a scrim of milky sclera. For a moment, I wondered what it must be like for a soul imprisoned inside the dagger. Was Gabriel Horne conscious and aware of his predicament, trapped in some never-ending nightmare?

I hoped for his sake that the answer was no.

I turned back to Archer. "You mentioned a message."

The detective nodded at one of the forensic guys and two members of the team gently turned the dead man over, almost as if they thought he was asleep and were taking great care not to wake him. My face fell as I saw the note that had been placed under the body.

It read: Don't try to stop me, Raven.

"Do you have an explanation for this?" Archer demanded.

The energy in the room had changed. Suspicious gazes now bored into me. If part of me had still held out hope that Celeste wasn't the one behind this murder, the message swiftly put an end to that foolish notion. She might be a victim, but she was also a killer. And she clearly didn't know me or understand what made me tick. The warning had the exact opposite effect on me. Instead of encouraging me to back off this case, I'd do everything in my power to bring Celeste down.

My gut told me that revealing the origin of the murder weapon wouldn't go over too well, but Archer was a shrewd detective and could smell a lie from a thousand yards off.

"You know who did this, don't you? Talk to me, Raven!"

I was still debating how to best answer Archer's question when I noticed the fog gathering outside the gargantuan bedroom windows. No one else was paying any attention to the clouds circling around the penthouse. Under normal circumstances, it wouldn't have caught my interest either, but the last twenty-four hours had taught me to be wary of the mist—and the inhuman entities that traveled under its cover.

I advanced toward the windows. With each successive step, the fog drew closer, almost as if responding to my presence. The mist hung over the building like a giant shroud. As my gaze searched the white-gray cloud, I vaguely made out slithering shapes.

"Archer, tell your men to move away from the windows," I said, my voice holding a note of urgency.

"What's going on?"

"Let's say I have a hunch that things are about get ugly."

No doubt about it—shadowy shapes were moving inside the swirling mist. That was never a good thing. Archer picked up on it too. We both had witnessed enough weird shit to know that something was up.

"What is it?" she asked. "Raven, damn it, if you're somehow doing this...."

Before I could offer up an explanation, a tentacle thrashed out from the fog and slammed into the window next to my head, cracking the glass. The cops and forensic guys in the room jumped.

"Raven?" Archer asked, her voice shaky.

The tentacle withdrew. I sensed the movement it created beyond the glass pane.

The hellhounds were preparing to attack again.

The supernatural fog was serving as a bridge between worlds, just as it had outside the coffee shop.

During its first attempt to manifest, the tentacle had appeared ghostlike, more like a shadow, but with each passing moment it was gaining substance. The next time the monstrous appendage lashed out, the glass would shatter and all hell would break loose—and I meant that in the literal sense.

The events at the coffee shop were still fresh in my memory. If the hellhounds seized control of the cops in the penthouse...let's just say a mass possession would lead to a lot of innocent people getting hurt.

Good people, like Benson and the baby-faced forensics kid.

And Archer.

I pivoted and walked briskly away from the damaged window.

"Raven, where are you going?" Archer asked.

"I have to leave. For all our sakes."

"What are you talking about? What's going on here?"

Good question. A part of me wanted to come clean and tell her everything. I caught myself in time. I couldn't involve Archer and put her in harm's way. The less she knew, the safer she'd be.

"The fog is after me," I said after a pause that went on a beat too long.

Archer grabbed my hand. Her touch was electric. "What is going on here?"

"It's my problem."

"Wrong answer. This is all our problem."

Archer had a point. But I didn't have time for this. I pulled back from her and turned away. I felt her eyes digging into me as I left the apartment. I almost had something special once with Archer, but I blew it. I'd be lucky if she ever spoke to me again. Hell, I'd be lucky if she didn't shoot me the next time our paths crossed.

My footsteps echoed as I left the penthouse at the swift pace of a man who knew the forces of Hell were hot on his tail.

10

They always say that in case of an emergency, you should use the stairs. I tore down the back stairs of Gabriel Horne's building three at a time. This pack of hellhounds was smart enough to mess with the elevator if I tried to use it, and the thought of hurtling down twenty stories in a metal coffin was more than enough motivation to hoof it to the lobby.

As soon as I reached the street, I looked up toward the penthouse. The thick clouds had fully enveloped the building and now drifted with malevolent intent down the sidewalk.

Toward me.

High time to get my ass in gear.

I surged back to my car and made it inside without any further surprises. The cloud picked up speed, and started to roll toward the Equus Bass. I cranked up the engine and punched the gas, and soon the supernatural bank of condensation receded in my rear-view mirror.

I considered my next move. Celeste clearly intended to trade Gabriel Horne's soul for her own, but would the demon accept her counter-offer? I doubted it. Celeste's soul was more valuable to the demon than her half-brother's. If only a fraction of the tabloid stories were true, the scion of the Horne family was a bad boy on steroids. His soul was probably hellbound already.

If this exchange was going to work, Celeste would have to sweeten the deal somehow. Hell would only let her go if they received something of greater value than her soul. In other words, she'd have to make them an offer they couldn't refuse. If she couldn't deal in quality, she would have to settle for quantity. That suggested the soul blade would need to seek out more victims before the day was over.

It was all beginning to make sense in my mind. Celeste had the worst daddy issues I'd ever encountered. Killing off his legitimate heirs was an unmistakable plea for attention from the father who had abandoned her—and it just might get her out of the devil's bargain, too.

With Gabriel dead, only two Horne kids remained. Eric was the older of the two, while Robert was closer to Celeste's age. That was where my knowledge of the Horne clan ended. It was time to call Skulick.

He answered on the first ring. "How did it go? Is Detective Archer giving you a hard time?"

I'd never told Skulick about what had happened between Archer and me, but I didn't have to. Skulick, sly and perceptive bastard that he was, had a sixth sense about that kind of stuff.

"Can we please talk about the case and not my personal life? The hellhounds immediately picked up my scent. I barely avoided an incident at the crime scene."

"Where are you now?"

"Just driving, trying to stay mobile while I figure out my next move. My guess is Celeste is going to go after another one of Horne's children."

"My thoughts exactly. According to the news, Eric Horne cut his Toronto business trip short and is on a flight back to the States. As long as he is on a plane, he should be safe."

"What about Robert Horne?" I said. "Does he work for their father's company, too?"

"No, he's the black sheep of the family. An up-and-coming artist who has gone on record denouncing his father's media empire but doesn't seem to have any problems accepting cash from daddy when he needs it."

"Any idea how I can find him?" I wanted to know.

"Looks like he rents a space downtown where he

lives and works."

"Sounds familiar." I guess Skulick and I weren't the only one whose work was their life.

"A local art magazine apparently considers his art to be both challenging and transformative, whatever that means. Bet it looks like a kid painted it."

The words put a smile on my face. There was no pretense or fake affectation when it came to my partner.

"Okay, I'm going to pay him a visit—hopefully before Celeste does," I said.

"Sounds good. I'm sending you his address now."

My cell chimed, and juggling the phone in one hand, I plugged the address into my navigation app.

"On a related note," I said, "Do you have any intel on how Desmond Horne is taking the news of his oldest son's murder?"

"No comments from his camp yet. He's has been ill for weeks now and hasn't been seen around his midtown office building. Scuttlebutt is that he's sequestered in his estate about fifty miles outside the city, which also happens to be surrounded by an army of trigger-happy bodyguards."

In other words, good luck getting within a hundred yards of the Horne patriarch. "Okay, I'm on my way to Robert's now. Keep me posted if anything else should come up."

"You got it, kid."

I smiled. "Thanks, boss."

Skulick hung up, leaving me to my own thoughts. I touched the mark of the demon on my chest and wondered why the scar hadn't detected the hellhounds for the second time in a row. My scar was sensitive to all supernatural activity, as far as I knew, and it had never failed me before. So what was different about the demonic force inside the mist?

No matter how hard I racked my brain, the answer to the maddening question kept eluding me. I cranked up my stereo, and a loud rock anthem filled the Bass 770. The music helped blank out my mind. Screeching electric guitar solos and pounding drumbeats swept all dark thoughts of demons aside.

I arrived at the art gallery less than a half an hour later. Feeling refreshed by my music therapy session, I climbed out of the car and walked up to the rundown two-story gallery. Nearby, a freeway cast a shadow over the neighborhood, the incessant traffic forming a steady soundtrack in the background. Further off, there was a McDonald's and an exotic nightclub, its neon sign dead in the dull gray daylight. I figured Robert's art had to be pretty special if well-heeled buyers were willing to trek out to this forsaken part of the city.

There was no trace of the supernatural fog here, and

I wondered how long it would take for the hellhounds to find me. I had to act fast. Hopefully I'd be able to convince Robert that I was here to help—and that I wasn't insane. Trying to convince a stranger that his long-lost half-sister was coming to kill him with a magic knife would be a hard sell.

Mind and body alert, I pushed open the glass double doors and entered Robert Horne's art gallery. A pervasive silence hung over the space. I stood in front of the empty reception area for a few moments, unsure where to go next. It seemed rather careless to leave the space unattended in a shady neighborhood like this one. My sense of unease deepened as my hand wandered toward my shoulder holster. The scar on my chest wasn't giving off any warning signs, but that clearly meant little.

When no one showed up after five minutes, I decided to explore the gallery on my own. The reception room led into a long corridor, and I followed it deeper into the building. I passed through the door at the end of the hallway and stepped into a sprawling, high-ceilinged exhibition space.

The lights were on, so surely somebody had to be here. My gaze combed the space, and I received my first taste of Robert's gritty street art. Unsettling graffiti murals and sculptures defined the exhibition room – apparently Robert worked in multiple mediums. Long-limbed, spindly creatures, part reptilian and part insectile, featured in the compositions, grotesque shadow beasts artistically brought to spooky life. A giant maw of fiery red teeth covered one wall, while another sported a collection of glaring eyeballs. The lifelike quality of the pieces suggested the artist hadn't pulled them completely from his imagination. Some of the graffiti murals dotting the exhibition space looked like distorted reflection of demons I'd faced in the past. The man was using his art to work through something. Like his father, the dark side apparently exerted a strong pull on Robert Horne.

I was beginning to understand why potential clients would make the pilgrimage to this rundown location. These pieces exuded raw, uncompromising power and would be catnip to the right one-percenter with a dark sensibility and cash to burn.

I edged deeper into the space. The shadows of the statues lengthened, the light hiding more than it revealed. My footsteps echoed, and the sound made me nervous. *You're walking into a trap*, my inner voice told me, and I drew *Hellseeker*.

Gun ready, I weaved around another sculpture and froze.

I'd found Robert Horne.

11

The lifeless body, eyes blank and white as his brother's had been, lay sprawled beneath one of the unsettling canvases. He'd become the centerpiece of his own grisly art exhibit.

I inspected the gore-caked chest and found the three puncture wounds of the Soul Dagger. I touched the body, and the skin felt warm. Robert hadn't been dead for long.

I slowly turned away from the corpse as I realized I wasn't alone in the art space. Celeste was still here, standing about fifteen feet away from me, crimson-sheathed blade in hand. I guess I'm a sucker for a pretty face and a lady in need of rescuing, because until I saw her with the murder weapon, part of me still hoped that she'd somehow turn out to be innocent.

"Don't make that face," she said. "I bet this isn't the first dead body you've seen in your line of work."

Wasn't that the truth.

"He didn't suffer. One moment he was here—an obnoxious, self-important, and self-hating carbon foot-print—and the next..."

She held up the knife, and wiped the blood off with a rag.

"His soul now belongs to me to do with as I please." She sounded like a giddy sixteen-year old who had just gotten her first car. "One final sacrifice awaits. Three souls should make for a fair trade, wouldn't you agree?"

Shaking my head, I said, "You really think the creatures you want to bargain with will play fair?"

"Maybe I'll throw dad in for good measure," she said. Her pouty lips were painted dark plum today, but her punk-rock goddess chic no longer worked on me, not now that I knew what she was.

I took a step toward her, *Hellseeker* leveled at her heart.

"I thought you only killed supernaturals," she pointed out. "I'm human, Raven. You wouldn't hurt me, would you?"

"You're a practitioner of the dark arts," I said.

"Is that how you justify murdering me in cold blood?"

"Just drop the knife."

"What if I don't?" Her features lost their playfulness, growing defiant. "We don't have to be enemies. Walk away, Raven. Go back to hunting your werewolves and mummies and whatever. This isn't your problem."

"That knife belongs to me. And you're using it to kill people. Therefore, it *is* my problem. Plus I'm still a little upset about the time you knocked me out and then marked me with your blood."

"You can handle yourself, Raven. The hellhounds will figure it out soon enough and back off."

"You lied to me."

Her lips stretched into a tight line. "I had no choice. Time's running out for me. I need to be ready for when the bargaining begins in earnest."

"Good luck with that," I said, revolted by how cold and calm she could be about all of this.

"The Horne boys were born with a silver spoon in their mouths. Always taking without giving back anything. I won't spend an eternity burning in Hell so a bunch of spoilt brats can live out their privileged lives while their stock portfolios grow." She took a step closer, a fiery intensity in her voice, "I never asked for this, Raven. Any of it."

"I don't care what you asked for. You're a murderer, and I'm not letting you walk away from it. Robert and

Gabriel had nothing to do with the deal your father made."

"Are you sure? Don't you think they knew what was going on, that their perfect lives were built on the pain and misery of countless innocent people? Look around! Robert's art speaks for itself, doesn't it? I think he will feel right at home in Hell."

The mad logic of her words affected me. On some level, I understood her need for vengeance. That's what fueled my own decision to keep the world safe from paranormal threats. Yet there existed a critical difference between Celeste and me. I was trying to avenge the murder of my parents by hunting monsters while Celeste had become one herself, seeking revenge by slaughtering innocents. If anything, her rage should have been directed against the man who'd betrayed her in the first place.

"I'm sorry about what happened to you. Together, we could've found the way to—"

"Ever the knight in shining armor. Sorry, Raven, I'm too old to believe in fairy tales. Nowadays I make my own luck and work my own magic."

Magic has already blackened your soul, I thought wearily.

Celeste placed her palms together, and her eyes narrowed into slits as her lips mouthed silent words.

She was casting a spell. My protective ring grew hot to the touch, sensing that a new attack was imminent. My finger hovered over the trigger, but a voice inside stopped me from shooting Celeste before she could complete the spell. She was right about the code by which I lived my life. I had no qualms putting an end to demons, but Celeste was human.

I couldn't shoot her. But I couldn't let her go, either.

I holstered *Hellseeker* and sprinted toward Celeste. Her lips moved faster, driven by a greater urgency to complete her magic. I threw myself on top of her, and she brought up the Soul Dagger. I'd anticipated the move and grabbed her wrist as we both crumpled to the floor. The knife sailed through the air. She tried to push me off her, but my weight kept her pinned to the ground. Her eyes flashed with fury, and she spat into my face.

Why can't I ever meet any nice girls?

Before I could respond, I sensed a large figure approaching with swift strides behind me and spun toward my phantom attacker. Too late! A supernatural force snatched me and unceremoniously lifted me into the air. I dangled about ten feet above Celeste, airborne and helpless, her laughter echoing in my ears. Without warning, the force released me, and I went flying. I clenched my jaw as I crash-landed, knocking over one of Robert's monstrous statues in the process.

The sculpture shattered on impact. Pain shot through my back but shock masked most of it. Between the Blackmore Witch and this latest craziness, my body was taking one hell of a beating. By tomorrow I would be covered in nasty bruises—if there was going to be a tomorrow.

A nightmare creature loomed above me. One of Robert's graffiti creations was peeling itself away from its canvas, haunting art turning into a nightmarish reality. The painting—a devilish creature defined by jagged line work—gained form and substance, a two-dimensional image come to life.

To the left, a second painted creature followed. The image in question—a grotesquely elongated, spiked shadow—joined the first and closed in. Both the shadow and devil turned to me in unison. Reality rippled and shimmered around them, Ceeleste's magic struggling to maintain their consistency. I had faced demons and living nightmares but never anything like golems made from spray paint.

The first creature had caught me off guard, but I wouldn't let that happen again.

I whipped out *Hellseeker* and fired. The bullets hit the two graffiti monsters, and the magical creations reared up with bestial moans. They were no match for my blessed weapon and dissolved on impact in a cloud of paint, splashing back toward the murals from which they'd come. Their monstrous bellows gave way to a silence broken by my own heavy breathing.

I searched the exhibition space and realized Celeste was gone.

The spell had never posed a real threat; it was meant to distract me long enough to give her a chance to escape. I spun toward the exit and was about to run after my charming former client when a roiling cloud of fog cut me off. Spreading mist blanketed the space within seconds. As the fog engulfed the sculptures and graffiti murals, I feared the entity or entities traveling inside the mist would crib a page from Celeste's magical playbook and imbue Robert's art with an unnatural life.

I killed the thought. This wasn't the time to let my imagination run wild.

Something shifted in the mist.

A silhouette grew visible in the swirling clouds of unnatural condensation. The stench of sulphur assaulted my senses as the mist fully encircled me. Without warning, Robert's body lurched from the gray cloud, his steps halting and jerky. The demon had possessed the dead man, using Robert Horne's corpse as his ride.

Before I could give him a taste of *Hellseeker*, the undead monster was upon me. The reanimated corpse brusquely knocked my blessed pistol from my hand. The gun clattered across the floor.

I was battling an actual zombie demon, and my scar still hadn't given so much as a twinge. *What was going on here?*

The answer would have to wait. Steel fingers closed around my throat and lifted me with inhuman strength into the air. My feet dangled inches above the floor. The possessed corpse let out a roar of triumph. Robert's slack, empty features hovered right above mine. The zombie-demon's foul stench made my stomach lurch. A forked tongue danced between bluish lips, offering a glimpse at the demonic creature hiding inside the dead body.

The white eyes roamed over my face, taking in every detail. The beast reminded me of a dog sniffing its trapped prey, a final ritual soon to be followed by the killing blow

"You're not the soul promised to my master," the hellhound whispered. *"Where is the one we seek? Answer me, mortal."*

I wanted to tell the thing to go to Hell, but in this case it would be redundant. Instead I asked the question that had perplexed me since first meeting Celeste.

"Who is your master, hellspawn?"

The zombie's lips twitched and a terrible grin split his face.

"You're not the soul promised to my master, but he's met you before."

"What?" I blinked at it, perplexed. Generally speaking, when I faced a demon, one of us didn't walk away.

"Don't you already know?"

The voice had changed. The new one made the first one sound almost childlike in comparison, its confident intelligence and sense of absolute power undeniable. There was something familiar about it. I was gripped with a sudden horrific suspicion.

"We met a long time ago, Raven. Don't tell me you've forgotten? I sure haven't forgotten you. Or your parents." The creature let out a peal of laughter and a cold shiver of dread crawled up my spine. It couldn't be. It was impossible.

My eyes flitted to the walking corpse's shadow. The silhouette painted across the floor wasn't human but belonged to a nightmare creature straight out of the deepest pits of Hell. Massive batlike wings extended from a broad back, framing an elongated, horned head. Whirling tentacles undulated from the thickly muscled torso and lashed the air.

I knew that form. It belonged to the creature that still haunted my nightmares.

I finally understood why my scar hadn't been able to detect the demon's approach. The demon hunting Celeste was the same monster whose mark I bore on my chest. After sixteen years, I was finally facing the demon who'd slaughtered my parents.

12

I owa, *21 years earlier.*

Snow fell outside the boy's bedroom window. Wide-eyed and open-mouthed, young Mike Raven marveled at the winter wonderland that had sprung up overnight. Christmas decorations twinkled in the night, a constant reminder that the holiday was only a few weeks away at this point. There was a red glowing Santa astride his sleigh, pulled by sparkling reindeer. Further off, near the dense woods enclosing the property, stood an inflatable snowman family.

Mike Raven had lived the first eight years of his life in Los Angeles, and this was his first experience of what his dad called a "real winter." To say that he was excited would be an understatement. He couldn't wait for tomorrow to arrive, when he would finally explore the snow-blanketed world beyond his window.

His father had promised to help him build a snowman come the next morning and his stomach fluttered with happy anticipation. Dad's job as a traveling salesman kept him on the road for most of the year, and Raven didn't see him that often. This Christmas was going to be different though. In Raven's young mind, this was definitely shaping up to be the best Christmas ever.

He kept his face pressed against the cold windowpane, and his breath left smudges on the glass. Despite his eagerness for the day ahead, sleep was catching up with him. A yawn escaped from his lips, and his eyelids grew heavy. It was an hour past his bedtime already. He was about to crawl back under the covers when his gaze locked on a strange shape outside. At first he wasn't sure what he was staring at. As the shape drew closer, details became visible and his heart hitched into his throat.

The weird figure advancing toward their home was made of snow cast in the form of a human silhouette. Flakes danced around the inhuman figure as it slowly turned its featureless head toward him. Raven grew stock still, terror keeping him rooted. He wanted to back away from the window, but his body refused to cooperate.

"Dad," he croaked in a tiny voice.

To his growing horror, more snowy shapes emerged

from the frozen yard. The snow golems shared little in common with the smiling, carrot-nosed snowman family billowing happily in the wind nearby. These creatures were blank-faced and boasted muscular, threatening physiques.

Monsters aren't real, Raven thought.

He was about to learn otherwise.

"Dad?" he repeated. He was still paralyzed with fear, but his voice sounded stronger.

A loud bang rattled his bedroom window, and he jumped back. A shrill scream escaped from his throat as a snowy fist punched the window a second time. Glass turned to ice and shattered. A sharp gust of air blew into his room, snowflakes hitting his face. Raven let out another piercing scream and fled his bedroom.

Terrified, he surged down the hallway. His breath coming in uneven, panicky bursts, he screamed, "Mom, Dad!" He pushed open the door to his parent's bedroom.

Eight-year-old Raven stopped dead in his tracks. For a beat, he struggled to process what he was seeing. His mother's body lay splayed across the bed. Her skin was an unnatural blue, covered in frost, the eyes open wide and the lips frozen in a rictus of a scream. His mind went blank, shock stunning him into silence. Later on, the tears and nightmares would come, but right now there was only a deep-seated numbness.

Something moved in the dark bedroom. One of the ice creatures emerged from the shadows, menacing and alien. Raven's terror gave way to raw anger. He would kill it. The nightmare creature had hurt his mother, and he would tear the thing to pieces. As the figure lurched toward him, his father's voice filled the bedroom. "Raven, get down!"

Somehow his dad's voice cut through his paralysis, and he hit the floor face first. There was a loud crack, and then a bullet punched into the inhuman assassin. Tufts of snow exploded from the entry point and the snow creature went supernova, a red aura of fiery heat enveloping its form. The next moment the ice golem fell apart, the magic animating the snow rendered ineffective. Where his mother's killer had stood, there was now only a pile of black, watery sludge.

Never again would Raven find much beauty in winter, or snow, or even Christmas. It would always make him think about the tragic day when his childhood ended.

A strong arm reached down and pulled him back to his feet. In his father's other hand was a glowing green pistol. Somehow, he understood that the weapon's magic had destroyed the snow monster.

"Listen carefully, son. Our home is surrounded by

those creatures but I'm going to keep you safe. I won't let them hurt you."

Raven looked up at his father and nodded. The man was dressed in a bathrobe and wore his favorite plaid pajamas underneath. There was something different about his dad's face, though. A dark fire burned in his eyes, and he seemed almost...dangerous. This wasn't the face of a traveling salesman but of a hero from the movies. Raven had never seen his father like this.

The sound of breaking glass reverberated through the house. At least one of the lethal ice creatures had made it inside.

"Come on, move!" his father barked. "I promise we'll make it out of here. Do you believe me? Answer me, son!"

Raven nodded again even though he didn't know what he should believe at this point.

Gun out, his dad whisked him through the living room. The lights of their Christmas tree cast multicolored shadows, adding a surreal touch to their escape. Some part of the boy's mind still believed this was nothing but a nightmare. They'd decorated the tree only a few days earlier. How could it be possible that his mom was now lying dead in the other room? Any minute now, he'd wake up and smell the pancakes she always cooked for breakfast on special occasions, and then they'd open presents and sing songs and have a snowball fight, and everything would be right in the world.

A window shattered nearby. Raven whirled to see an ice monster as it pulled itself into their living room in a flurry of snow.

His father's gun blazed, the crack both deafening and reassuring. The ice golem exploded in a cloud of snow. Another lurched from the kitchen, icicle fingers glittering red in the Christmas tree lights. Another quick shot from *Hellseeker* reduced the beast to a puddle of melting snow.

His dad's fingers dug deep into the boy's hand as they ran. More windows exploded, and Raven tried to remember how many of the creature he'd spotted back in the yard. There had to be more than ten. How many bullets did his father have?

Up ahead, the hallway ended in the door leading to the garage, where his father's treasured black Plymouth Barracuda was parked. The car had always reminded him of the Batmobile, and Raven sometimes imagined that his dad was a superhero out fighting crime instead of a boring vacuum cleaner salesman. Now he was starting to wonder if his fantasies had been right all along. His dad flung the hall door open, and together they raced down the stairs and ran for the car. Loud crashing noises drifted from above, but the monsters seemed to be intent on tearing the place apart rather than following them.

His father tore the Plymouth's passenger door open and helped Raven get inside. He pulled the seat belt over him, the buckle snapping in place with a resounding click.

"Brave boy," his father said and patted his cheek. For one brief moment, the monsters ceased to be of importance. Raven felt proud, as if the two of them could overcome any challenge. Just like Batman and Robin.

The door slammed shut, and his father clambered in on the driver's side. The engine revved, a beast coming to snarling life.

"Hang on!" his father shouted.

Dad floored the gas, and the Plymouth tore through the flimsy garage door. Two snow monsters appeared seemingly out of nowhere and launched themselves at the vehicle. Raven cried out as the two bodies thumped against the moving Plymouth. To his surprise, strange symbols lit up along the windows, reminding him of the colorful lights of their abandoned Christmas tree. The creatures reared back from the lights as if hit by an electrical charge and transformed into splashing puddles of water that streaked down the windshield.

The car's speed increased as they whipped down the driveway.

Raven relaxed just a fraction. They were getting away. His dad had saved them, just like he promised.

Houses blurred past them as his father navigated the Plymouth down a series of winding roads. As the snow-blanketed world rushed past the Plymouth's window, Raven could only think of his mother's frozen, lifeless form. His dad might have saved them, but all help had come too late for her. Screeching tires pulled him out of his disturbing thoughts. A wall of fire lit up the night, blocking the road ahead.

His dad's features darkened. A shadow eight feet tall rose from the ring of flames, a creature straight from the depths of Hell. Later, Raven would learn that the snow monsters had been the first wave of the hellish attack, mere hellhounds that could take on various forms or possess the living. The entity ahead was different. This was one of the Dukes of Hell, a full-fledged demon.

His father slammed the brakes, and the car screeched to a halt inches away from the flames. The demon grinned, and a long, tentacle-like tongue flickered out from between its teeth. The tongue whipped through the air toward the Plymouth's windshield. With a crackle of mystical energy, the sigils and glyphs powered up, but the magic failed to prevent the attack.

With the precision of a laser beam, the tip of the tongue dug itself into the soft flesh of the boy's chest. Blood spurted and agony exploded through his little body as he went into shock. Instinctively, he fought back against the urge to close his eyes and block out the horror and pain. He knew if he passed out, he wouldn't make it out alive.

From the corner of his eye, he saw a knife slicing down. The blade severed the tip of the tongue, and black blood splashed Raven's face. The sticky fluid burned his skin, the stench over-powering.

Whip-fast, the damaged tongue withdrew back into the monster's mouth. With a roar of rage and pain, the demon's wings flared out, and he launched himself at the Plymouth. The boy's father never showed any fear. That was what he would remember most about this moment. Not his own terror or pain, but the calm, steady gaze of his father as he told Raven to run and never look back.

Raven could only nod, hot tears streaking down his face. His dad released the seat belt and handed him the green glowing gun.

"The gun will keep you safe. Use it the way I taught you. NOW RUN!"

Raven didn't remember taking *Hellseeker* or opening

the door. Didn't remember climbing out of the car. Didn't remember breaking into a run.

He only recalled what happened next.

His father cranked the engine, and the Plymouth blasted toward the demon at full crank. Raven did go against his father's wishes and turned his head as he ran, watching the scene unfold.

The demon rippled toward the incoming vehicle. Gunfire filled the night, his dad blasting away as he charged forward in a suicide run. Even at eight years old, Raven understood that his father was buying him time to get away—and the currency for this distraction would be life.

Raven stumbled to a halt. His heart hammering with terror, he watched as the Plymouth slammed into the demonic figure at full speed. Later he would remember his father winking at him just before the impact. He must've imagined that part, his memory playing tricks, but the image persisted. As he grew older, Raven drew a weird comfort from it, this final positive memory of his father to hold on to.

Metal twisted and buckled as the Plymouth erupted into a fireball that lit up the blustery winter night. Heat singed Raven's face; roaring fire surrounded the demon. It seemed to be laughing. An instant later it disappeared, returning to whatever hellscape had spawned it.

Suddenly there was a new sound, a roaring, unholy noise that seemed to bash against his ears. Raven's head slumped forward and his body sagged, all strength leaving his limbs. Whatever terrible thing was heading toward him, he no longer had the strength to run. The horrors of the last hour were catching up to him. He'd lost the two people that meant the most to him in the whole world in the same night.

Instead of a new supernatural threat, a familiar man walked over to Raven and gazed at the burning wreckage of the Plymouth. Like his dad, he was sporting a glowing gun, his long trench coat flapping in the wind.

Raven looked up, his eyes blurred with tears.

"Uncle Skulick?" he asked, trying to make sense of what he was seeing. His father's best friend reached down and hauled him to his feet.

13

As the memories slashed through my mind, the past came alive in a rush of images and emotions. I gasped as the zombie demon threatened to crush my throat, and I clenched my fists to hide their trembling. Facing the demon made me feel like I was eight years old again, and the pain of losing my parents felt fresh.

As Robert Horne's reanimated *corpse* lashed out at me again, my instincts took over. I had one rule: I didn't take human lives. But I could use deadly force against the creatures of the night, be they vamps, weres, wraiths or any other form of supernatural nastiness. Robert was a zombie, his lifeless body a vehicle for the demon tearing toward me. Which made him fair game.

Even without *Hellseeker*, I still had a few tricks up my

sleeve. Without hesitation, I whipped out my demon slayer blade and slashed the zombie.

He recoiled with a wail, allowing me to wriggle away from him. I scrambled madly toward my downed pistol. With a desperate lunge, I scooped up *Hellseeker* and spun toward the demon. Blessed lead stitched Horne's undead form and drove him back. Had the creature chosen to physically manifest, I would've been done for, but within this corpse's shell he was too weak to resist *Hellseeker*. There are limits to the power of the blessed pistol, as my father and I discovered two decades earlier when we faced this same beast.

The hail of bullets from the magical gun flung Robert into one of the grotesque statues, a weirdly elongated and horned animal skeleton, and both the bullet-riddled body and the statue went down.

Smoke wafted from *Hellseeker*, and the stench of cordite burned my nostrils. My hand shook and I felt sick in the pit of my stomach. The demon's very presence had made me ill. I sucked in deep gulps of air and wiped the sweat from my face.

My brain was on fire; a myriad of questions dominated my thoughts. How could Celeste's situation be so closely tied to my own? Was it a coincidence that her soul had been promised to my parents' killer, or was there some connection or design afoot? A chilling thought occurred to me as I reviewed the timeline. Twenty-one years ago my parents had been murdered, about the time Celeste was born...

Dammit, I needed to talk to Skulick about this! Man did I miss having him with me in the field. This monster hunter business worked best as a team effort. Together we might come up with a working theory to explain this crazy connection.

Despite all our efforts, one question had tormented us for years: Which demon had targeted my family? Hell counted many assassins among its legions. I had always believed my father had pissed off the wrong horned bastard during his work as a hunter, but maybe there was a different explanation.

I scrambled to my feet and approached the downed zombie. Empty eyes peered glassily up at me, the demon's presence long gone. I resisted the temptation to kick the corpse for good measure. God, how I wanted to put the thing that had killed my parents in a world of pain. I exhaled sharply and balled my fists, struggling to maintain my composure. Pulling myself together, I tried to steer my thoughts into a more logical, constructive direction. Better to channel my rage against the real enemy. The dead man before me was a victim and had served as a convenient vehicle to the beast that had caused all this misery. At the stroke of midnight, the filthy beast would materialize in front of Celeste, and he'd find me waiting for him, guns blazing.

The sound of approaching footsteps pulled me out of my seething thoughts of vengeance. I whirled around and came face to face with Detective Jane Archer.

For a split second our recent awkwardness didn't matter as relief flooded me. I was so happy to see a familiar face. The moment didn't last long because her service revolver was pointed straight at me.

Archer was a good cop; she must've figured out the killer might make a go for Robert Horne next. And from her point of view, the corpse I'd pumped full of bullets wasn't a demon or monster but the son of one of the most influential men in the city.

Spending the night in a jail cell wasn't an option. Only a few hours remained before midnight. I intended to be there when the demon came for Celeste's soul. And there was still a chance of saving the last surviving Horne brother. Getting arrested at this point in the game would be a disaster.

"I know this looks bad, Jane," I said, my voice sounding meek to myself, "but there's an explanation for all of this."

"I'm listening." There was a strange calm in her voice, her features unreadable.

I pointed at the corpse at my feet. "Robert Horne was

already dead when I got here," I explained. "The stab wound on his chest matches the one of the other victim."

Archer ducked into her haunches and located the wound in question. A frown wrinkled her forehead. "So why pump an entire magazine into him?"

"Would you believe me if I told you a demon hitched a ride in Robert Horne's corpse and took a swing at me?" I said with a sheepish grin twitching at the edges of my lips.

Archer considered this for a beat. To my surprise, she coolly said, "Can't really blame him."

I clenched my jaw. "This isn't funny."

"Neither is murder." The playfulness had gone out of her voice, icy now.

"You know me, Archer," I implored, spreading my hands wide.

"I thought so at one point." Her gun never wavered as she spoke. All business.

Despite the gun leveled at me, I took a step toward her.

"You have to trust me on this, Jane."

The professional exterior cracked, and the knot of muscles on the side of her jaw pulsed. "Last time I *trusted* you, it didn't work out so well, did it now? To be honest, I don't think I'm the one who has a problem trusting people."

Touché.

"I'm sorry, Archer. I really am. I never meant to hurt you."

Her eyes flickered, but her face maintained its steely composure. "You wouldn't be the first relationship-phobic guy looking for a quick fling."

Those words stung, but I deserved them. Archer was right. I avoided relationships, sure, but not for the reasons most guys do. Archer wasn't a one-night stand to me. I cared about her. And that more than anything terrified me. Every time I allowed someone into my heart, they were taken from me. If something were to happen to Archer because of me, because of what I do...

To my surprise, Archer lowered her pistol

"Tell me, why are the Hornes being targeted?"

"One of them made a deal with a demon, and Hell is about to collect."

"You got to give me more than that."

"I'm running out of time, Jane, and it's a long story."

Sirens were growing louder outside the art gallery. More cops were on the way. Any moment now, the place would be swarming with the boys in blue. I had to get out of here. Almost as if Archer had read my thoughts, she nodded at the exit.

"I believe you didn't kill this man, but once forensics

runs those bullets and traces them back to your gun, I won't be able to protect you."

"This isn't a normal gun. They won't be able to trace the ballistics."

Archer seem to think about the implications of this statement. "You're saying you have a magic gun?"

I shrugged. "It's a little more complicated than that."

"You want to know why I became a cop?" she asked, crossing her arms over her chest. "I wanted to make a difference, to put the animals that hurt the little guys behind bars. But this city has a bigger problem than crime, doesn't it? Let me help you, Raven. That's all I'm asking for."

"I'm public enemy number one to the Man Below. I don't think it's a good idea to get too close to me."

"As far as I recall, you once told me that no one is safe in a Cursed City."

"This isn't just your battle. Whatever is happening in this city, it's affecting everyone."

Damn, she made a lot of sense. And she looked far better than a woman who'd just been pointing a gun at me should. "You want to help? Look the other way and let me go."

"You can't fight this battle on your own."

She was right, of course. Fighting the forces of Hell wasn't a solo act. With Skulick out of the picture, I was vulnerable. I needed someone to cover my back. Could that someone be Archer?

She'd asked the right question, but the answer would have to wait. Even she seemed aware of this and stepped aside, nodding at the exit again. The sirens were deafening now.

"Go!" she said.

I took a step closer and fought the temptation to touch her shoulder. I caught a whiff of her perfume and flashed back to the passionate night we'd spent together. She stepped aside before I could make up my mind to try to reach out. I backed away and slipped through the art gallery's back door.

Archer had not completely forgiven me but maybe I could make things right in the future.

Sometimes all you need is hope.

Hope, a magic gun and enough ammo to make Hell take notice.

14

Night skulked the buildings as the city streaked past me. Noticing the Equus Bass' climbing speedometer, I willed myself to slow down. Getting pulled over at this point wouldn't help anyone. It would take about an hour to make my way to the Horne estate if I followed the speed limit. I hoped I would be in time.

The clock on the dashboard read 8:13 PM. By now Eric Horne must've landed at the airport and was probably on his way to his daddy's estate. According to Skulick's intel, the place was impenetrable, with both human and electronic security measures turning the property into a fortress. Celeste's magic would give her an edge. Fortunately, I wielded some supernatural firepower of my own.

The urban sprawl gave way to rolling countryside as

the city's skyline receded in my rear-view mirror. My phone rang, and I had a good idea of who it was before I picked up. I tapped the answer button, and Skulick's voice filled my car.

"Kid, I've been trying to get a hold of you for the last hour. The news is going nuts over the second Horne murder. Talk to me, what's going on?"

I felt bad for ignoring my partner's calls for that long, but I'd had my hands full. Zombies, graffiti monsters, attractive women trying to kill me, and confronting the demon that had killed my parents—it had been a busy day. "Robert Horne is dead. Celeste got to him first. And apparently low-level sleeping spells are only the tip of the iceberg of what she's capable of."

There was a beat of silence before Skulick said, "What do you mean?"

"Has a painting ever tried to eat you?"

"Well, there was that time in Scotland..."

My partner can be a real comedian at times but maybe he was telling the truth. The man has faced some crazy shit over the years.

"Never mind," I said. One thing's for sure. Celeste has been studying magic for years. And you know what that means?"

"She must've known about her father's Faustian pact long before she called us."

"My thoughts exactly," I said. We were on the same page here.

"Something else has been bothering me. How does a child raişed by a maid turn into a skilled spellcaster?"

I'd been asking myself the same question. There was only one possible explanation.

"She'd need a teacher and mentor to reach that level of skill," I said.

"Exactly. Perhaps in her frustration she conjured her own demon."

The thought of possibly having to go up against two of Hell's servants made my stomach churn.

"Let's say Celeste's story was true but she changed the timeline," I said. "She finds out about her father and starts looking into her options. She begins to study magic and ignores the risks to her soul. After all, the girl has nothing to lose."

"Still doesn't explain why she waited until the last moment to go after the Soul Dagger."

"Maybe she only recently found out about the relic."

I ruled out this notion as soon as I brought it up. The more I thought about it, the more I became convinced that we were missing a part of the puzzle.

"Maybe she lied about the date when the demon is going to collect her soul?" I wondered out loud.

"The beast's recent activity level suggests otherwise. And so does the velocity of her killing spree."

I had to concur with Skulick. There was a reckless urgency to these killings. Celeste was playing for keeps.

"There's something else I haven't told you yet," I suddenly said, surprised at myself. I had planned to keep the next part to myself, at least until I knew more. But Skulick has a way of drawing information out of me. Plus I needed to get this off my chest.

"I'm all ears," Skulick said.

My voice was empty of all emotion as I spoke. "I confronted the demon back at Robert Horne's art gallery...and it's not the first time we faced him."

A deep silence greeted me on the other end of the line.

"We're up against the monster that killed mom and dad."

There ya go. The cat was out of the bag.

I tried to imagine Skulick's face during this moment. We both had spent more than a decade trying to identify my parents' killer and never gotten even close.

"Are you sure, kid?" Skulick said, his voice trembling with barely contained emotion. I think we'd both given up hope of ever avenging my parents. The denizens of Hell were many. As the years passed, new horrors had kept us busy and demanded our time and skill. Chasing after ghosts became a luxury when new monsters threatened the world every day. Still, the need for closure remained, like an open wound that refused to heal. Could this case be our chance of putting the past behind us?

"If that's true, do you know what it means?"

I had a theory. It was crazy, but *everything* about this situation was crazy. I decided to share it with Skulick.

"Horne might not have offered up his daughter's soul for the reason we thought," I said. "Maybe he wanted the demon to kill my parents. It would mean Horne didn't conjure Mammon or one of the other wealth demons. Instead, he must've summoned one of Hell's assassins to do his bidding."

"What would a media tycoon like Horne have to gain from your parents' death?" Skulick asked, giving voice to the myriad of crazy thoughts simmering inside of me.

The question hung there.

"This is absurd," Skulick acknowledged.

"No shit. But that doesn't mean it isn't true."

"And if Horne did target your parents, what are the odds his daughter would seek us out twenty-one years later by chance?"

"Somewhere south of zero," I said. "There's something we're not seeing here."

"You'd better return to headquarters," Skulick said. "I'm getting a bad vibe about all of this."

"Sorry, but no can do," I said. "I'm on my way to the Horne estate."

"Listen, kid, I can only imagine how this must be affecting you. If it weren't for this goddamn chair, I'd be out there with you. You're walking into the lion's den without backup. Without knowing what game Horne and his daughter are playing...well, I'm afraid you're not going be walking back out again."

"I'm sorry, Skulick, but I have no choice."

There was a steely determination in my voice.

"Getting yourself killed isn't the way to honor your parents."

"I survived the demon once. I can do it again."

Talk about an idle boast; Skulick had saved my sorry ass that night. Nevertheless, I needed to pump myself up for the upcoming confrontation. I had to believe I was doing the right thing here.

"Even if you find the answers you're looking for, how will you be able to destroy this demon?"

"That's why I'm going to interrogate Horne. Only he knows what we're dealing with here and why my parents were targeted."

And I want to look into the bastard's eyes before I pull the trigger, I mentally added. Out loud, I said, "Wish me luck."

With these words I killed the call. The renewed silence weighed heavy on me. Outside the car's windshield, the tree cover grew denser. Under normal circumstances, I would've tried to enjoy the bucolic view. For city boys like me, the country always had a special charm.

But not tonight. I barely noticed anything other than the stretch of road unwinding ahead of me.

Skulick was right. I was rushing into battle. But this wasn't a suicide mission, at least not in my mind. I had a plan. I would infiltrate the property and seek out the bastard who'd ordered my parents' murder. Soon, Desmond Horne would have to answer for the crimes of the past.

And if I found his answers lacking...well, maybe it was about time I broke my cardinal rule. I wasn't going to let the old bastard get away with my parents' murder.

15

Less than an hour remained before the demon, whose name I still didn't know, would claim Celeste's soul. I wouldn't be surprised if she was already at the mansion, waiting to strike her bargain when the demon materialized at midnight.

Of course, that was assuming the demon was sticking to this time zone. For all I knew, it might be operating on Tokyo time. But I didn't think so. Horne had made his bargain in the Cursed City. Celeste had found me here. Every sign pointed to this being the locus of whatever bad shit was about to go down.

Desmond Horne's mansion was still about a quarter of a mile away, but I couldn't drive closer to the property without the risk being spotted by the security team. A stranger wearing an increasingly rumpled trench coat doesn't quite blend in with the woods, but I had a plan.

Architectural Digest recently ran a piece on the estate, and I'd gleaned some helpful information from the article. What amounted to a small army patrolled the mansion and surrounding wild park around the clock. Odds were good that I might run into one of Horne's armed men before I even got close to the wrought iron gate.

In fact, I was counting on it.

I popped open the Equus Bass' trunk and opened the titanium case stashed in the back. A white mask sculpted to look like a horned monster stared back at me. It was made in the style of traditional Noh theater masks, and according to Skulick it had belonged to a fourteenth century Japanese mage. If you're asking yourself why I was about to don an ancient Japanese mask while trudging through the forest, I can assure you I had a perfectly logical explanation for my odd behavior.

Noh masks were carved from cypress wood and had to be light since performances often lasted for hours. The mask did make my skin itch and limited my peripheral vision somewhat, but if my plan worked, it would all be worth it.

As I moved through the dense underbrush, I kept thinking of my last visit to the countryside. Staring at the bare trees ahead, my mind cycled back to the poor campers who'd succumbed to the Blackmore Witch's horrific magic. Was Celeste destined to end up like the witch in the woods, nothing more than a twisted, evil creature corrupted by magic? I doubted she'd spare me on our next encounter. For the upcoming round, I wouldn't allow misplaced sentiment to hold me back.

After about a half an hour, I sensed movement nearby and grew still. The crackle of a walkie-talkie told me a guard was zeroing in on my position. The foliage parted, and a man sporting a gun emerged from the bushes. Black fatigues encased his muscular physique, and pair of cunning eyes surveyed the area from a meaty, florid face.

I looked at the man through the magical Noh mask, really took in the details of his roughly chiseled visage, before I stepped up to him. The man pivoted, and his weapon found me. There was a moment of surprise that gave way to shock and a trace of horror. Running into your doppelganger could have that effect on the most hardened individual.

The mask's magic had allowed me to copy the guard's appearance. To the outside world, I would be: *Bob Cohen, former Special Operator turned gun for hire, currently employed by Desmond Horne.*

Before the real Bob Cohen could gun me down, the palm of my hand snapped out and karate chopped his throat. His eyes rolled up as the oxygen supply to his brain was cut off, and he dropped to the ground face first.

The history of my magical Noh mask had been lost to time. Some legends claimed some mad thespian had turned to magic in the hopes of achieving the ultimate performance. I'd acquired the item while hunting a group of vampire ninjas under the control of the undead samurai Makaze, and I hadn't exactly taken the time to find an owner's manual for the artifact. What I did know was this: far more than a mere magical disguise, the wearer of the mask could access the vital information of the person they were impersonating. Don't ask me how it works; there's a reason they call it magic. I now knew everything Bob Cohen did about the estate, from the entire layout of the Horne property to the various security routines and names of the other guards. Pretending to be someone else could get you only so far. Knowing your enemy's secrets—now that was true power and the key to a successful infiltration.

I scooped up the downed man's walkie-talkie and gun and continued toward the house. Ten minutes later, I arrived at the grim, imposing Horne mansion. The sprawling home was constructed in the Gothic style with solid, polished columns and resplendent well-crafted moldings. The majestic facade exuded a malignant, sinister quality. It felt like it belonged to a different time and place.

I pressed through the gate and exchanged a few quick words with the other guards I came across. The mask modulated my voice, making me sound like the man I was impersonating. Even the all-seeing eyes of an electronic surveillance system would be fooled by the mask's magic. To the world I was Bob Cohen, member of the Horne security team.

A collection of luxury cars that looked like a car thief's wet dream were parked in the cobblestone driveway. I passed a few other armed guards, and they waved at me, seemingly pleased to see good ol' Bob. Despite the intimidating appearance of the man whose identity I'd momentarily borrowed, he appeared to be popular among his co-workers.

My walkie-talkie crackled as I walked up to the mansion's main entrance. *"Five-Nine to base. We have a problem!"*

There was panic in the guard's voice. Had one of the security guy's stumbled upon the real Bob Cohen? I turned around and my pulse hitched. A thick fog was forming around the property, the tendrils of yellowish condensation everywhere. All too soon, the mist would engulf the estate and seep into the mansion.

The demon was approaching fast. I checked my watch. Thirty minutes until the fireworks began.

The fog wasn't after me this time, which meant Celeste was already in the mansion. I shouldn't have been surprised, but I cursed inwardly. I'd been playing catch-up with her ever since our meeting back at the coffee shop. She was displaying a real knack for always being one step ahead of me.

With a renewed sense of urgency I strode into the Horne mansion. No one paid me any attention as I navigated the endless corridors. I was a familiar face doing my job of keeping the Horne home safe from anyone foolish enough to breach its defenses.

Oh, the irony.

The closer I got to my goal, the more my blood began to boil. I was eager to confront Desmond Horne and hadn't pondered what would happen beyond that point. To be honest, the dark emotions seething within me scared me. What would I do once I stood before the man who had destroyed my life?

I would know soon enough.

I paused when I reached an open doorway leading into what appeared to be a library. My scar had flared up. I bit my tongue, choking back the pain. The scar might fail to react to the demon that left the mark, but it easily picked up on Celeste's black magic. Letting my growing agony guide me, I entered the library. The space reminded me a little of the vault back at the loft. I kept moving deeper into the maze of shelves. After about a hundred feet, the pain in my chest intensified so much that I had to stop.

Up ahead, two guards stood by a table stacked with ancient volumes. A man sat leafing through one of the many tomes. It was Eric Horne. For once, I'd beat Celeste to the target. Eric must've hit the library as soon as he arrived at his father's estate. Judging by the occult titles of the tomes around him, he was trying to make sense of her murder spree—and he knew the killer had something to do with the supernatural. Strangely enough, neither the guard nor the youngest Horne, acknowledged my approach.

A moment later, I understood why they were ignoring me. All three of them were dead. The guards sported cyclopean third eyes where bullets had punched through their foreheads. A crimson circle soaked Eric's Horne shirt, and his white eyes stared life-lessly into space. Closer inspection of the wound would undoubtedly show a three-pronged scar from the Soul Dagger.

What gave the scene such a grotesque quality was that Celeste had used an animation spell on these three latest victims, conjuring the illusion of life to the casual observer. My scar was reacting to the black magic electrifying the air, but if a regular guard walked past the library and happened to hazard a glance inside, nothing would seem out of order. Eric Horne simply kept flipping pages, puppeteered by Celeste's unholy spell.

A walkie-talkie hissed, and one of the guards responded in a monotone voice. The sophistication of the spell served as a sharp reminder of what I was up against here. Celeste must've delved into the mysteries of the dark arts for years to pull something like this off. That easily accounted for her disregard for life. She'd murdered her three half-brothers and was clearly willing to add anyone who got in her way to her growing hitlist. Magic was great in theory, but when practiced by humans, its corrupting influence soon infected the thoughts of the practitioner.

These men would still be alive if I had acted faster, been smarter about all of this. I fought back the guilt. This wasn't the time for doubts and self-recriminations. I had failed to save the Horne brothers but maybe I could still spare their immortal souls an eternity in Hell.

I scanned the library and wondered where were Celeste and Desmond Horne were. By now, Celeste would know the demon was closing in on the Horne estate.

After a moment's contemplation, I realized there was

only one place they could be. Celeste intended to confront the demon in the same place where her soul had been bartered twenty-one years ago. They would be below, in the unholy temple Horne had built beneath his mansion. The only real question was how I could get down there.

Struck by sudden inspiration and guided by the steady throbbing in my chest, I regarded the bookshelves in front of me. With a little luck, my scar might lead me straight to Celeste. It was about time the thing did something useful on this case.

Allowing my pain to show me the way, I wandered like a blind man through the library. After about ten minutes, I stopped in front of a shelf where the dull ache in my chest was at its most pronounced.

This had to be it! The entrance to the temple. I touched the books with the ring of protection. With a flash of magical energy, the *Seal of Solomon* ignited and the bookshelf evaporated into thin air. The secret doorway to the temple stood revealed.

I pulled open the door and entered the dimly lit space beyond. Stone steps disappeared into the darkness. I unholstered *Hellseeker* and began to descend the winding flight of stairs.

The pain in my chest intensified with each step. I'd expected a single flight of stairs but the stone steps ran much deeper. As I walked in darkness, I lost all sense of time. At last, I arrived at a doorway framed by two flickering torches. This was it. I opened the wooden door, steeled for the worst.

As far as sites of human sacrifice and demon worship went, I'd seen worse. Torches ran along the walls, offering their scant light and heat. A winged demonic statue loomed at the far end of the temple and formed the centerpiece to this unholy place of worship. A rough-hewn stone altar fronted the idol of evil. Drawing closer, I recognized the man tied to the altar— it was Desmond Horne.

The final sacrifice, I thought.

He was wearing pajamas and an expensive silk nightrobe and looked like he was trying for a role in a Hugh Hefner biopic. Clearly his attacker must've caught him off guard in his home.

Guard up, I approached the altar. More details of the statue jumped into view. It was a good rendition of the beast I had first laid eyes upon when I was eight years old. I snapped a picture of the statue with my phone and tried to send it to Skulick but failed to get a signal in the subterranean temple.

Desmond Horne's wild eyes spotted me, and he desperately strained against the thick ropes holding him down. A gag made it impossible for him to say anything.

To Horne, I appeared to be one of his loyal guards who'd arrived in the nick of time.

I walked past him. My gaze probed the temple's shadows, looking for Celeste. My efforts were quickly rewarded as she stepped from behind the demonic idol.

"You can take off that silly mask, Raven. Your disguise can't fool me."

There was a beat of hesitation before I complied. The expression in Desmond Horne's eyes changed from hope to panic as I reverted to my usual self.

"It's midnight," Celeste said. "Looks liked you arrived right on time for the big show."

16

I didn't need to check my watch to know that midnight was upon us. The demon was near. Ever since I set foot in the temple, my whole being had been gripped by a sense of animal panic. Despite my years of hunting monsters, the demon's approach was affecting me in a primal way. The hair on my arms stood up, and my stomach cramped with anxiety. For a moment I was just prey reacting to an approaching predator.

Weirdly enough, replaying my first encounter with the demon allowed me to ride out the waves of terror. Like so many times before, thinking about my dead parents and the beast that had taken their lives turned my fear into anger.

Your chance to face the demon has come. Dad, Mom— today your killer will pay for his crimes.

The torches flickered inside the temple, and the shadows grew more menacing.

"You can feel it, can't you?" Celeste said. "He's here. Any moment now, we'll know if Morgal will accept my terms."

Morgal. The name sent an electric a jolt through me.

For years, the demon had just been an abstract boogeyman. Now my parents' killer had a name. It channeled my rage and anger, gave it a specific target. For the first time, closure was a possibility.

But first, I had to make it through the night alive.

Knowing the beast's name was only the first step. Without Skulick's knowledge of demonology, there was only one other person in the world who could tell me what I needed to know to defeat this monster. And this man was tied to the altar in front of me.

Muffled sounds of violence rang through the temple and brought my musings to an end. Bursts of machine gun fire echoed from above, followed by screams. I pictured the fog spreading into the mansion, down the long corridors, into the library and ultimately making its way down the secret stairway leading into the temple, all the while unleashing the hellhounds on Horne's security forces. They didn't stand a chance against the horror inside the hellish mist.

I focused on Celeste. "I don't think your father sold

your soul to Morgal in exchange for power and money. Your soul was payment for a hit on my parents."

If Celeste was surprised by this latest revelation, she didn't show it. Her gaze remained fixed on me.

"I want to know why Horne wanted my father out of the picture."

"Maybe we can ask Morgal himself?"

At the renewed mention of the demon's name, a wind rose and an arctic blast blew through the underground temple, extinguishing the torches for good. For a split second the temple was drenched in darkness. I felt a shape passing through that blackness. As it brushed past me, the beast's hot breath raked my neck. Then the light returned—muted and unnatural, magical in nature, but at least I could see again.

Morgal stood in the nave of the chapel about fifteen feet from my position. Ghostly tendrils of mist swirled around him. He had taken human form now, dressed in a long trench coat like myself.

As the fog cleared, I saw to my horror that Morgal hadn't dressed himself up in just any human form. He wore my father's face.

"You've made quite a name for yourself in Hell, Raven. Daddy would be so proud."

The skin bubbled and burned, turning to ash before being blown away by a supernatural gust of air. Now the face had become a blackened death skull, the eyes sockets raging with green-blue fire, the coat transformed in a long, tattered robe that shifted around his form as if alive.

The demon is messing with your mind, I told myself. *Just stay calm, Raven. Don't forget why you're here.*

After that mental pep talk, I tried to draw *Hellseeker* and found myself rooted in place, unable to move my legs or arms. I couldn't even speak. Somehow Morgal's magic had overcome my protective talismans with ease and paralyzed me.

Frustration boiled inside of me. My parents' killer stood less than fifteen feet away from me, and I couldn't even ask the demon why my folks had to die that night.

As the robed skeleton walked past me, tentacles squirmed under the robe and a pair of giant, batlike wings sprouted from his back. The demon's appearance remained in a constant state of flux, switching back and forth between a black death skull and a reptilian, horned face. Smoke and mirrors, I realized. Playing on our fears and nightmares. Who knew what the demon truly looked like under its many disguises?

"First, I'm going to collect the prize promised to me," Morgal said. "Then I'll deal with you, Raven."

I didn't want to picture what "dealing with me" meant. I needed to find a way to break out of my paralyzed state before it was too late. Morgal closed in on Celeste while I continued to watch helplessly. If the demon accepted her deal, Celeste would murder her father and I'd never discover why my parents were forced to pay the ultimate price. Then again, as soon as Celeste was done bargaining for her soul, Morgal would do with me as he pleased. The demon would delight in the knowledge that I'd perish without ever receiving any answers to my questions.

I should have listened to Skulick when he'd told me to come back to the loft instead of following Celeste. I'd let my emotions cloud my actions. Driven by my own need for closure and vengeance, I'd put myself at mortal risk and would now have to pay the price for my foolishness.

Morgal tilted his ever-shifting visage toward me, and said, almost as if he'd read my mind, "How does it feel to be so close to the answers to all your questions, Raven... yet so far away?"

God, how I wanted to unload *Hellseeker* into this monster. If I could just find a way to break my paralysis...

"That's far enough, demon," Celeste said. Morgal had almost reached the altar.

"You dare tell me what to do?" Morgal said. "Your soul belongs to me, mortal."

"I offer a trade, mighty Morgal."

"What is this foolishness, child? You want to cheat me out of a contract?"

"Not cheat, master. Offer better terms."

Celeste held up the Soul Dagger and the demon stopped his approach. The light in the ebony skull's eye sockets flickered, as if he was blinking in surprise.

Morgal might be powerful, but he wasn't all-knowing. This was an unexpected turn of events for the demon. I could only hope that it would help me in the long run, but at the moment I didn't see how.

"The dagger contains the souls of my half-brothers, and I'm willing to add this waste of space," she pointed at her father, "if it sweetens the deal. They can all be yours, Lord of Lords, Master of Magicians, Duke of Hell. Four souls in exchange for my own."

"What stops me from taking the dagger and your soul too?" the demon retorted.

I had been asking myself the same question. Celeste was playing a dangerous game.

"Only the person who took these lives can release them from the blade. If you want them, you need me."

Morgal considered Celeste's words. "How do I know if you're telling the truth? You could be bluffing about the dagger."

She shrugged and held out the Soul Dagger. "Feel free to inspect the blade."

Morgal reached out a skeletal hand across the altar. Desmond Horne squirmed between them, Morgal's inhuman shadow falling over his face.

Celeste passed Morgal the dagger, and the demon studied the ornately carved handle. Blue forks of lightning danced over the blade as it made contact with the beast.

"Do you believe me now?" Celeste said.

"You speak the truth, yet this bargain holds little appeal to me," Morgal said. "These souls were already tainted and hellbound. How can you claim to give me what is already mine?"

Celeste's eyes flicked toward me. The negotiation was slipping away from her.

I had suspected the demon might react like this from the start. Celeste would have been better off murdering innocent people beyond Hell's reach, like the Berlin Ripper had done. But she had allowed herself to be blinded by her hunger for vengeance. Denied her father's love and attention all her life, she'd targeted the siblings who'd never had to suffer the way she did.

If I'd been in her place, I'd have found some nuns or orphans to offer up. Barring that, I would try to find a specific person whose soul the demon craved. Somebody who'd really pissed off Hell. Somebody like me.

Suddenly I had a good idea where this was headed.

Celeste's next words proved me right.

"How about I turn the blade against Raven, Hell's biggest enemy? Imagine how your status will grow when his soul is your trophy. A knight of the light doomed to spend all eternity in darkness. With Raven out of the way, the Prince of Darkness will be able to continue his conquest unchallenged. Imagine what rewards he will grant you."

Morgal's eyes narrowed as they locked on me. If I made it out of this alive, Skulick and I were going to have a long talk about vetting our clients to make sure none of them were malicious, double-crossing, murder-happy thieves.

"You *could* kill Raven," Celeste said. "Torture him, put him through every misery imaginable. But ultimately his body will give out. Only the blade you now hold can give you his soul."

The demon nodded and his leathery wings flared out, casting jagged shadows against the temple walls. The skull-face had changed again, now a reptilian devil mask.

"Done," he said. "You have yourself a deal, child. If

you take the blade and strike down Hell's greatest enemy, your soul will be spared."

With these words, Morgal handed the Soul Dagger back to Celeste. I braced myself for the inevitable, still paralyzed, unable to raise a hand in my defense. In a way, I couldn't even be angry with Celeste. The girl was a survivor. She would do anything to live—or so I believed. What happened next showed me that I had gotten this whole thing wrong yet again.

As soon as Morgal handed Celeste the Soul Dagger, she brought it up to her chest and drove it into her heart. Blood gushed from the wound, and her hand slipped off the dagger's hilt. I couldn't believe what I was seeing. Even Morgal appeared aghast.

Celeste collapsed on top of the altar. While I was still trying to make sense of what had just happened, Desmond Horne threw off his restraints and snatched the bloody knife from his daughter's corpse.

The helplessness and despair was gone from his face. Despite his advanced age, this was the predatory, relentless man I'd studied back in Skulick's loft. This whole thing had been a set-up, but what was the old man's ultimate goal?

As this latest insight spun through my mind, Desmond Horne brought up the Soul Dagger and drove it with all his might into Morgal.

17

The blade sunk into the demon's inhuman flesh.

For a brief yet timeless moment, reality froze, the yawning silence deafening. Morgal backed away, his reptilian expression stunned that a mere mortal would dare defy him in such an impertinent manner.

A beat later, the world sped up as Morgal's ferocious roar shook the temple. He clutched the Soul Dagger's ivory handle and withdrew it from his gut. The artifact clattered to the floor, the three-bladed dagger slick with the creature's black blood.

"How dare you, mortal?" Morgal roared, his slitted eyes fixed on his new enemy. "I'll make you suffer like no member of your species has ever..."

Morgal broke off as a series of tremors tore through

his body. His whole form began to tremble and shake. The red-black eyes turned a sickly white, and streamers of spectral light enveloped his form.

Desmond Horne rose from the altar and surveyed his handiwork with a look of deep satisfaction. For the first time, I wondered who I should fear more: Morgal or Horne?

My eyes shifted back to my parents' killer. In the violent display of light flickering around the demon, I made out human shapes and faces.

Understanding slashed through my mind. I was looking at the spirits of the three Horne brothers as well as Celeste. Desmond Horne had released their trapped souls when he stabbed Morgal with the Soul Dagger. The spirits were now inside the demon, battling over control for the monster's form.

His inhuman physique reared and bucked. As he stumbled down the temple's nave, giant wings sliced the air and tentacles lashed out furiously, knocking over pews. The demon's monstrous limbs did not move under his orders any longer. The puppeteer had become the puppet—but who was in the driver's seat?

The souls of Horne's children were battling it out to see which one would control the demon. Horne himself just watched, cold and calculating, as Morgal fought against their attempts at possession.

What game was the Desmond Horne playing here?

Morgal roared in fury and pain as the four souls pulsed around him, becoming a blazing tornado of supernatural light. The demon could've easily crushed one soul foolish enough to attempt such an impossible feat, but four seemed to be enough to give him a challenge.

My mind was reeling. Had Desmond Horne sacrificed his children because he believed their souls could successfully take control of the beast? I doubted very much that would work so what did the old man hope to gain?

Morgal dug a clawed reptilian fist into his glowing chest. An instant later, the talons emerged from his body, now clutching a squirming ghost. It was Eric Horne's spirit form.

The demon popped the spirit's head like a balloon, fragments of screaming ethereal energy dispersing throughout the unholy temple.

One soul down, three more to go.

I sensed this struggle wouldn't go on for much longer. Four human spirits weren't powerful enough to possess a demon for any length of time. Already, Morgal was reasserting control. The outcome of this battle was a foregone conclusion. Desmond Horne had miscalculated, and his gambit would fail within the next few minutes as the souls of his children were defeated.

I eyed the old man. His features were still calm and composed, but a flicker of triumph in his narrowed gaze gave me pause. What was the old devil up to?

As if to provide an answer to my question, Horne began to recite an ancient prayer. An arcane magical circle lit up around the altar. A series of glyphs appeared inside the circle, previously invisible to the naked eye.

The demon tore another one of the attacking souls from his heaving body and shredded it. Robert Horne's spirit mouthed a silent scream as the demon's incredible power tore his soul apart.

Only Celeste and Garbriel remained, their spirits flickering dimly inside the demon's struggling form. They were growing weaker. As their ranks had thinned, their struggle intensified.

Horne's voice rose as he chanted, swelling with power. A second magic circle ignited around Morgal, identical to the one Desmond Horne stood in. More arcane symbols grew visible, both inside the circle as well as the walls and ceiling of the underground temple.

That's when I finally understood what was happening. I'd been wrong about everything. So very, very wrong.

This isn't a place of worship, I realized. *It's a trap.*

Celeste Horne's soul had been the bait to lure the demon into this temple. And the four souls were meant to both distract Morgal and steer him into the previously invisible magical circle. Horne had never believed his kids could defeat the demon. Their deaths were just another part of his game.

Morgal was coming to the same conclusion. "What is this?" the demon cried as he pulled Celeste's soul from his mouth and crushed her in his clawed hands. I got one final look at the femme fatale who'd played me from the start. There was no fear in her eyes as her soul perished, only an expression of ecstatic triumph.

Celeste had lied to me on so many levels. She'd never been the disowned bastard child out for revenge. The dark devotion expressed in her final moments spoke volumes. She had been a loyal servant, dedicated to carrying out her father's plans. I was witnessing the culmination of a long con that had lasted more than two decades.

While these thoughts cycled through my mind, Morgal tried to escape from the magical circle by hurtling himself against its borders with all his might. There was a crackle of mystical energy, and blue-green forks of electricity arced as the invisible force field repelled the beast.

Even a demon couldn't overcome Desmond Horne's spell.

"What have you done, human?" Morgal demanded to know.

Desmond Horne offered no answer as his chant built into a raw-throated cry. I made out snippets of Latin and Aramaic but the nature of the spell eluded me.

The two magical circles changed color, the white light turning an electric blue as Desmond Horne's occult ritual hit its crescendo. Blinding rays of light licked the air. Under normal circumstances I would have shielded my gaze from the furious light, but my paralysis forced me to keep watching.

Supernatural energy washed over the demon's monstrous features, the eerie light flooding his mouth full of razor-sharp teeth, saturating his scaly skin. Morgal slumped to his knees, his monstrous head hunched forward, a Duke of Hell bested by a mere mortal.

If I hadn't seen it with my own eyes, I would never have believed it.

The violent bursts of magical energy dispersed in a final blinding flash.

Reality was back to normal.

Well, almost normal.

The magical circle around Morgal still pulsed with a steady red light. I still struggled to grasp the point of this ritual. What had Horne hoped to accomplish here? The demon might be dead, but after everything he'd done, Horne's soul was most assuredly doomed to an eternity in Hell regardless.

The cry of absolute horror that followed was my first clue. This time, the pitiful scream hadn't originated from the demon but from Desmond Horne. The old man was on his knees, mirroring Morgal's expression of defeat. The circle around the altar shone with the same muted crimson energy as the circle ringing the demon.

"No, it can't be. This is impossible!" Horne cried in despair.

Had Horne's spell misfired? Had he spent the lives of all his children for nothing? I still struggled to make sense of the old man's intentions and the nature of his crazy ritual. If Skulick had been here, he would have figured it out.

Desmond Horne stared in abject horror at the demon's slumped body and then his own limbs, his wild-eyed gaze darting back and forth at a frantic tempo.

"What have you done, mortal?" he asked, his voice cracking.

The demon's head lifted then, and it began to laugh.

I finally grasped what had happened here, what

Desmond Horne had been after all along. The old bastard had indeed achieved his goal.

As Morgal stumbled erect, triumphant laughter bursting from the hideous maw rimmed with razor-sharp teeth, I knew. And so did the pitiful old man trapped inside the magical circle surrounding the altar.

Except, of course, that the old man was no longer Desmond Horne.

Somehow, he had managed to switch bodies with the demon.

Morgal's soul was now trapped inside the frail, sagging anatomy of a seventy-year-old man while Desmond Horne controlled the demon's mighty form.

Neither Hell nor Earth would ever be the same again.

18

S ince the beginning of time, men had dreamt of becoming gods.

To someone like Desmond Horne, turning into a demon was the next best thing.

The demon aimed its terrifying gaze at me. The wings unfurled as it took an unsteady step, Horne's soul still learning how to operate the monstrous anatomy.

He was getting the hang of it fast.

"Do you finally understand?" the Horne demon said. "Has your pathetic little brain caught up?"

I understand that you're a madman, I thought, still incapable of forming words.

"If you lose, you're a madman. If you win, you're a visionary genius," the Horne demon retorted in response to my thoughts.

And he can read minds. That's just fantastic.

"I will make you pay for this, Horne!" Morgal screamed inside Horne's body.

The Horne demon turned toward his former self. "Choose your words carefully, Morgal. You know how sensitive human nerve endings are to pain."

"My master will never let you get away with this!" Morgal said, rage mixing with mounting panic. "Hell will see through this deception and the Prince of Darkness will punish you for your boldness."

"Perhaps you're right," Horne conceded. "But I don't intend to deceive anyone. Hell will know what I've accomplished. The Prince of Darkness won't shed any tears over a demon foolish enough to be tricked by a human. Especially when I hand them Raven's soul on a platter."

It made a sick kind of sense. Desmond Horne would buy his way into Hell's aristocracy using my soul as his currency. His plan was so audacious that it just might work.

From the furious expression on Morgal's wrinkled features, the demon had come to the same conclusion. His fury drove him to try stepping out of the magical circle. Energy sizzled, and he bounced back as if he had run into a concrete wall. The demon collapsed, out for the count.

"I can't image what poor Morgal must be going through," the Horne Demon said. "To trade such power for my old, broken body...it must be like being buried alive in a coffin made of flesh and bone."

The Horne demon regarded me and the paralysis lifted slightly. I could feel my face again, and my lips immediately formed words.

"How long...were you...planning this?" I said, still struggling to form words. My tongue felt sluggish, and my mouth was painfully dry.

"Since my sweet, loyal Celeste was born," he said.

Since you had my parents murdered, I mentally added.

"Twenty-one years ago, I was secretly using my cult to expand my business operations. My followers would infiltrate the companies of my greatest competitors, causing them to thrive or fail on my orders. Your father and his partner knew something was up and were closing in on my operation. I was at a crucial phase. My power and influence were growing, but a couple of idealistic do-gooders could've ruined it all."

"So you conjured Morgal and got him to kill my mother and father." My voice trembled with emotion.

"Yes," Horne said without a trace of remorse. "I assumed that if one of the demon hunters was dead, the other would stop chasing me. I thought that targeting the family man would be more effective, so your father's fate was sealed."

Rage burned inside of me, and my heart hammered with hatred.

"In a way, I ought to thank your father. The moment I first laid eyes on Morgal, everything changed. I finally understood that my earthly ambitions paled in comparison to the demon's power. A new idea took root inside of me, an idea that would dominate the next two decades of my life. What if I could become a demon myself? With your father and his partner out of the picture, my worldly empire grew, but it meant nothing to me anymore. No matter what I achieved on this mortal plain, death would come for me sooner than later. But if I could become a demon, I would be eternal. Far better to serve in Hell than to rule on Earth, don't you think?"

The bastard thought he was being cute by riffing on the classic line from *Paradise Lost*. I concentrated on broadcasting the worst insults and curse words I could think of in Horne's direction. If he really could read my thoughts, then he'd know exactly what I thought of him.

The Horne demon's lips crinkled into a sharp-toothed smile. "I'll take that as a compliment. I never felt like I belonged to this world; the dirt, the blood, the sweat and tears seemed beneath me. My body a flawed vessel doomed to shrivel and perish. Becoming a demon would be the ultimate act of transcendence, pulling myself up from the muck and leaving this crude matter behind for something far more glorious."

He paused, his wings sweeping the air with greater control and precision.

"I needed to seize control of Morgal's power the next time he manifested himself. That gave me twenty-one years to set the perfect trap for the demon."

The insane extent of Horne's plan, the crazy level of dedication it had required, started to dawn on me.

"You raised your children to be part of this madness," I said out loud. "Your sons as well as your daughter. Brainwashed them until they were your soldiers, willing to blindly make any sacrifice required from them."

In my mind's eye, I replayed the murders of the three Horne sons but this time Eric, Gabriel and Robert all helped guide Celeste's hand as she pierced their hearts with the Soul Dagger. They had offered up their lives and souls to aid their father's insane quest to become an even greater monster than he already was.

"My offspring served only one purpose—to pave the way for my transformation."

"You led them to their deaths," I said. "Parents are

supposed to love and protect their kids, not use them as pawns in some sick game."

"We all die, Raven but we don't all truly live. Their sacrifice wasn't in vain, and they were glad to make it. They believed in the plan, and as you can see, everything worked out perfectly in the end."

For you, you old bastard, I thought. *But what about them?*

Another insight occurred to me.

"It was you who taught Celeste magic."

"I felt it might come in handy as we neared the day of reckoning."

I considered this and asked, "How did you know about the Soul Dagger?"

"I kept close tabs on your father's work, even as he tried to hunt me down. I read the reports on the Berlin Ripper case."

The Horne demon took a step toward the edge of the still-glowing circle but didn't pass beyond its boundaries.

"I'd always feared we might not be able to contain Morgal in the magical circle long enough for our souls to successfully switch bodies," he continued, clearly pleased to have a captive audience to hear all about his triumph. If I could just keep him talking, maybe I could find a way out of his mess.

"You needed a distraction."

"That's correct. The Soul Dagger would allow them to attack Morgal in a way that would throw him off balance and allow me to successfully complete the ritual. For my plan to succeed, I needed to retrieve the blade."

"Then why not just steal it? Why bother going through the whole charade with Celeste asking for our help?"

"I didn't know if Hell was monitoring my actions. Morgal had to believe that Celeste's offer was real so he would let his guard down. That scar on your chest connects you with Morgal. It's why I can read your mind now, Raven. I knew he'd scan your thoughts once he entered the temple, and if you were convinced that Celeste had betrayed you, he would have no reason to be suspicious of my daughter."

"So you wanted me to be here for all this? It was part of the plan from the beginning?"

"I leave nothing up to chance. You were always the key, Raven. Especially for what follows next."

The Horne demon held up the Soul Dagger, the implication clear. He would hand deliver my soul to the Prince of Darkness.

"It's fitting," Horne said, "that your father's death

opened my eyes to my true destiny, and now his son's death will assure I fulfill it."

Horne had waited for this moment for twenty-one years.

But so had I.

My eyes remained riveted on the two magic circles, which had changed color from blood red to electric blue. Horne still hadn't attempted to leave the ring of glyphs, and I guessed that the soul transfer spell hadn't quite run its course. Horne's victorious rant couldn't disguise the fact that he hadn't actually won yet.

Over the course of my conversation with the Horne demon, the *Seal of Solomon* I wore on my index finger had grown hot as it ate away at the magic holding me in place. I already sensed some feeling gradually returning to my hands. My anger was breaking through Morgal's paralysis spell, or maybe swapping souls with the demon had weakened the magic. I couldn't be sure. But I liked to believe that my love for my parents and my need to avenge them played an important role in what happened next.

Tapping into my rage, I kept focusing on my hand. I moved my fingers inch by strenuous inch while I visualized pulling off the ring with my other hand and throwing the *Seal of Solomon* into Horne's protective circle. I replayed this image over and over again, all the while masking my thoughts with the very real anger I still felt.

I sensed Horne was catching psychic impression of my thoughts, and his demonic eyes lit up with sudden alarm. But by then it was already too late.

I saw my mother's frozen form, her bluish lips, her wide-open eyes staring emptily into space.

I saw the roaring flames consume my father's car as he slammed into Morgal.

I saw myself, a young orphan lost in a world of horrors.

Horne had taken my parents from me, and with them any chance I'd had at a normal life. My rage exploded and movement returned to my body. In less than a second the ring was off my finger.

"No!" Horne said.

Yes.

I hurled the ring into Horne's magic circle.

The *Seal of Solomon* clearly didn't like Horne's magic too much as the circle went from blue to a searing, almost neon yellow.

And then the circles were gone.

Judging by the terror in the old man's wizened features, interrupting the magical ritual had sent his soul back to his ailing human body.

Morgal regarded me for a beat. Had I just made the biggest mistake of my monster-hunting career?

Instead of attacking me, Morgal inclined his head a fraction of an inch in thanks to me and then turned toward the man who'd dreamt of being a demon.

"Please." It was the only word Horne managed to say before the demon launched itself at him.

19

Flesh was Morgal's canvas, pain his muse. The demon had spent eternity figuring out new ways of torturing the damned. Considering the horrors he was willing to inflict on random strangers, I couldn't imagine what was in store for Horne.

The next few moments gave me a gut-wrenching preview.

Morgal tore into the old man and went to work. Horne's cries of agony soon devolved into animal squeals. Horne had become a screaming piece of meat, and Morgal was both butcher and surgeon working him over.

Mercifully Morgal's large wings enveloped the altar, sparing me the details. I don't have the stomach for torture even if it is well deserved.

With Morgal focused on his grisly handiwork, I cut a hasty retreat. More than anything else in the world, I wanted to face the demon in battle, but I didn't stand a chance against this agent of darkness. Confronting him without a more powerful weapon than *Hellseeker* was suicide. My best bet was to get out of here so I could fight another day.

Relieved to be in charge of my body again, I made my way toward the magical circle that had served as Morgal's prison. Horne's haunting screams intensified as I retreated.

I stopped in front of the circle and swiftly retrieved both the *Seal of Solomon* and the Soul Dagger. Crouched at the edge of the circle, the low angle offered me a view of Celeste's dead body next to the altar. The sight filled me with sadness and pity. She'd never had a chance. Horne had molded and manipulated her since birth, used her as a means to an end on his mad quest for power. Just one more victim of the man's out-of-control ego.

I slipped the relics into the deep pockets of my coat and continued toward the stairs. I didn't get too far before Morgal became aware of my escape attempt. I froze as the demon turned his reptilian visage toward me. We looked at each other. *Into* each other. No words were exchanged, but the expression in those nightmarish, bottomless eyes sent chills down my spine.

The demon returned his full attention to Horne. The message was clear. Morgal would spare me today, but I sensed he wouldn't extend the same courtesy to me the next time around. I'd spared Morgal from a fate worse than death, and apparently there was some honor among demons. Or perhaps Morgal wanted to conserve his energy for the blood-caked old man on the altar.

Either way, there was a knowing smugness in the demon's gaze. Perhaps letting me live for now with my own demons was the greater hell. I had saved my parents' killer. That wasn't going to be easy to live with —and how was I going to tell Skulick?

There would be a rematch in the future, I was certain of that. I'd better be prepared for when our paths crossed again.

Turning away from the temple, I climbed the stairs, my muscles aching with each step, as Horne's death screams receded behind me.

My pace had picked up considerably by the time I reached the library. Outside the mansion, I heard wailing sirens. The cops were closing in on the property. Great. If Detective Archer showed up now, she might not believe I'd been an innocent bystander for these murders.

I passed Eric Horne and the dead bodyguards, who'd finally been allowed to rest. Eric was slumped in his chair, his blank gaze directed at the wall of books as if searching for an explanation for what had gone wrong here today. With Celeste's death, the animation spell stopped working.

Once outside the library, I stumbled through one hallway after another, the knowledge I'd gained from the Noh mask forgotten. The place felt even more oppressive and decadent than when I first set foot inside. The oil paintings, the marble sculptures—I found no beauty in these expensive objects. To me, they served as sharp reminders of Horne's insatiable greed.

Scanning the hallway ahead, I detected no signs of any guards. Horne's security team must've fled when the supernatural fog enveloped the property. At least I hoped they'd fled. A machine pistol makes for a poor choice of weapon against a demon.

The sound of approaching footsteps made me freeze. The police were here. I hid behind the main staircase that dominated the lavishly appointed front lobby. A beat later, the heavy oak door was rammed open and police officers swarmed the lobby.

I slipped on the Noh mask and focused on one of the incoming cops. As the officer passed my hiding spot, I emerged from the space beneath the staircase, now just another cop combing the scene.

No one paid me any attention as I slipped out the front door. I never looked back as I descended a set of stone stairs to the grounds below. I passed immaculate stretches of grass and perfectly trimmed hedges. Up ahead, a collection of police cruisers formed a barrier around the mansion. Sirens painted the night red and blue.

Archer was just getting out of her car. She met my gaze, and for a beat, I thought she could recognize me despite my magical disguise.

The moment ended as she rushed toward the mansion, not paying me any mind. Just wishful thinking of my part, I guess. After what happened in the temple, I wanted to fall into her arms, feel her heat against me. I craved human contact and connection, anything to release this maelstrom of emotions.

You chose the lesser of two evils, I told myself. Morgal was just the blunt instrument that had delivered the deathblow. It was madness to seek revenge against the weapon instead of the murderer. Horne was the one who had signed my parents' death sentence. Allowing him to gain a foothold in Hell would have been worse than sparing Morgal. Or at least that's what I tried to convince myself of as I walked away from the estate.

Numbed by the events of the evening, I stumbled through the woods and somehow managed to locate my ride.

I got into the car, fired up the engine, and drove back to the Cursed City in silence. I was in no mood for music. My hands shook, clinging to the steering wheel like a life raft.

Once back at the loft, I headed straight for the bar area. Instead of pouring myself a drink, I took a deep pull straight from the bottle.

As always, Skulick sat hunched before his bank of monitors, busy monitoring the web and media outlets for our next potential case.

"So, how did it go?"

I wanted to tell him the whole story but something held me back. Why reopen this old wound unless I could offer closure?

"It was Horne who ordered the hit on your parents, wasn't it?"

I stared at Skulick, stunned by my partner's uncanny insight.

"How did you know?" I asked.

"Used to be a detective, kid. Once you told me that Horne made a deal with the demon who killed your dad, I started doing some digging."

I nodded and took another swig. "Horne felt you and

Dad were closing in on his cult activities and figured that breaking up your partnership would make you back off."

I filled him in on the rest of the story, and Skulick listened quietly, his face betraying zero emotion. When I was done, he nodded at the bottle of Johnny Walker, and I poured him a generous drink.

He usually sipped his whiskey, but now he knocked it back in one swig. His voice quivered as he said, "I'm sorry, kid. I wish I could've been there with you when you faced these monsters. I'm so sorry you had to go through this on your own."

I walked over and put my hand on his shoulder. "I wasn't on my own."

I meant it. For twenty-one years, Skulick had been my protector and teacher, both father and friend.

I was the man I am today because of him.

His injury had changed our partnership, but we were still a team. And we had a new enemy now. Morgal.

"Don't keep beating yourself up. Next time we face the demon, we'll kill him. The bastard isn't getting away again."

Skulick patted my hand. "Your parents would be proud of you, Mike. And so am I. You make us proud every day."

There was a lump in my throat as I put the bottle of

Johnny Walker down and nodded at the bank of screens. Time to change the subject before I got too emotional.

"Anything happening out there?"

Skulick cocked an eyebrow. "Ever hear of Club Link?"

"Do I look like I have time for clubbing?"

Skulick winked at me. "Two hours ago, a couple was found dead there. Authorities have shut down the place while they investigate."

"Sounds like someone partied too hard."

"There were eyewitness reports of a strange figure in the club, a pale woman dressed all in white. It got my attention."

I was surprised to find myself up for another case after my run-in with Horne and Morgal. I guess I needed something to get my mind off what happened. Fast.

"So who is the woman in white?" I said.

"Two months ago, a model overdosed at the club," Skulick explained.

I soaked this in and said, "You're saying the ghost of a dead model haunts this club?"

"Only one way to know for sure."

"The fun never stops around here."

"We don't call it the Cursed City for nothing," Skulick said.

I cracked a smile. It was a little shaky around the edges, but it felt good to know I could smile at all after what had happened.

Morgal would pay for his crimes. In the meantime, our war against the supernatural went on. Monsters dwelled in the shadows of this city. It was up to Skulick and me to shine a light on the darkness.

THE END

Mike Raven and John Skulick return in SOUL CATCHER.

ABOUT THE AUTHOR

William Massa is a produced screenwriter and best-selling Amazon author. His film credits include *Return to House on Haunted Hill* and he has sold pitches and scripts to Warner, USA TV, Silver Pictures, Dark Castle, Maverick and Sony.

William has lived in New York, Florida, Europe and now resides in Venice Beach surrounded by skaters and surfers. He writes science fiction and dark fantasy/urban fantasy horror with an action-adventure flavor.

Writing can be a solitary pursuit but rewriting can be a group effort. I strive to make each book better than the last and feedback is incredibly helpful. If you have notes, thoughts or comments about this book or want to contact me, feel free to contact me at:

williammassabooks@gmail.com

facebook.com/WilliamMassaBooks

STAND ALONES

Fear the Light

Match: A Supernatural Thriller

Crossing the Darkness

.

Printed in Great Britain
by Amazon